BELIEVE THE IMPOSSIBLE

Every Sunday afternoon when Michael and I had dessert at the St. Regis, my mother and a friend had dessert and coffee there too. That way she could gossip or complain or conduct business but still keep an eye on me, without actually having to be *with* me. After the St. Regis, we would cap off our Sundays at Tiffany's. My mother loved diamonds, wore them everywhere, collected them the way other people collect crystal unicorns, or those weird ceramic Japanese cats with the one paw in the air.

Of course I was okay, those Sundays, because I had Michael for company. Michael, who was my best friend in the world, maybe my only friend, when I was eight years old.

My imaginary friend.

— From SUNDAYS AT TIFFANY'S

"What do women want? At this point in his career Mr. Patterson probably has a better answer than Freud did." — Janet Maslin, *New York Times*

"Entertaining…Readers looking for a romantic escape will enjoy [this book]."

— *Midwest Book Review*

"A love story with an irresistible twist."

— *Woodstock Sentinel-Review* (Canada)

Please turn to the back of this book for a preview of James Patterson's thrilling new novel, *MAX*.

Also by James Patterson

Sam's Letters to Jennifer
Suzanne's Diary for Nicholas

A complete list of books by James Patterson is on pages 329–330.
For more information about James Patterson, go to
www.jamespatterson.com.

Sundays at Tiffany's

JAMES PATTERSON *and*
GABRIELLE CHARBONNET

GRAND CENTRAL
PUBLISHING

NEW YORK   BOSTON

Grand Central Publishing Edition

Reading Group Guide Copyright © 2009 by Hachette Book Group
Author Letter Copyright © 2009 by James Patterson
Excerpt from *MAX* Copyright © 2009 by James Patterson
Copyright © 2008 by James Patterson

This Grand Central Publishing edition is published by arrangement with Little, Brown and Company.

Grand Central Publishing
Hachette Book Group
237 Park Avenue, New York, NY 10017
Visit our Web site at www.HachetteBookGroup.com

Printed in the United States of America

First Trade Edition: January 2009

10 9 8 7 6 5 4 3 2 1

Grand Central Publishing is a division of Hachette Book Group, Inc.
The Grand Central Publishing name and logo is a trademark of Hachette Book Group, Inc.

The Library of Congress has cataloged the hardcover edition as follows:

Patterson, James.
   Sundays at Tiffany's / James Patterson and Gabrielle Charbonnet.—
1st ed.
     p. cm.
   ISBN: 978-0-316-01477-9
    1. Imaginary companions—Fiction.   I. Charbonnet, Gabrielle.
II. Title.
   PS3566.A822S77 2008
   813'.54—dc22   2007031530

ISBN 978-0-446-19944-5 (pbk.)
ISBN 978-0-446-55463-3 (Scholastic Edition)

WHEN MY SON, JACK, was four, I had to make a trip to Los Angeles. I asked him if he was going to miss me. "Not so much," Jack told me. "You're not going to miss me?" I said. Jack shook his head, and he said, "Love means you can never be apart." I think that's the basis on which this story was built, and I suppose that it revolves around a belief that nothing is more important in life than giving and receiving love. At least, that has been my experience.

And so, this is for you, Jack, my wise son, with much love. And for Suzie—your mom, my best friend and wife, all in one.

And, finally, for Richard DiLallo, who helped tremendously at a key point in the development of the final story.

—J.P.

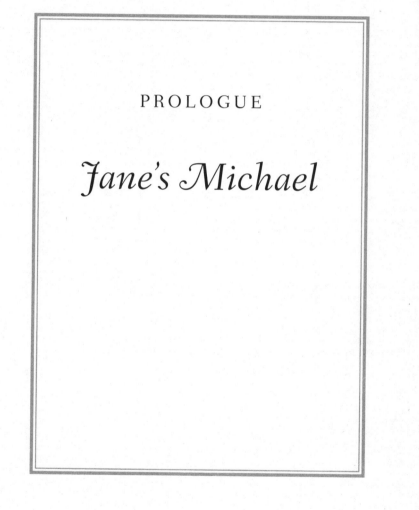

PROLOGUE

Jane's Michael

MICHAEL WAS RUNNING as fast as he could, racing down thickly congested streets toward New York Hospital—*Jane was dying there*—when suddenly a scene from the past came back to him, a dizzying rush of overpowering memories that nearly knocked him out of his sneakers. He remembered sitting with Jane in the Astor Court at the St. Regis Hotel, the two of them there under circumstances too improbable to imagine.

He remembered everything perfectly—Jane's hot fudge and coffee ice cream sundae, what they had talked about—as if it had happened yesterday. All of it almost impossible to believe. No, definitely impossible to believe.

It was just like every other unfathomable mystery in life, Michael couldn't help thinking as he ran harder, faster.

Like Jane dying on him now, after everything they had been through to be together.

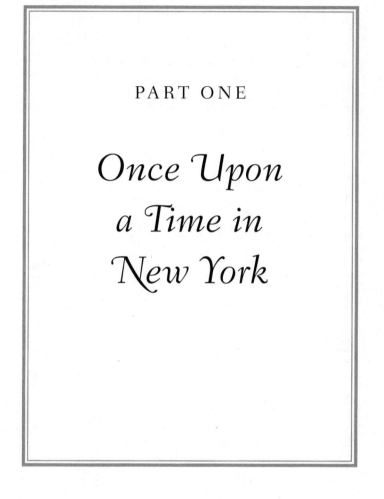

PART ONE

*Once Upon
a Time in
New York*

One

EVERY DETAIL of those Sunday afternoons is locked in my memory, but instead of explaining me and Michael right off, I'll start with the world's best, most luscious, and possibly most sinful ice cream sundae, as served at the St. Regis Hotel in New York City.

It was always the same: two fist-sized scoops of coffee ice cream, swirled with a river of hot fudge sauce, the kind that gets thicker, gooey and chewy, when it hits the ice cream. On top of that, *real* whipped cream. Even at eight years old, I could tell the difference between real whipped cream and the fake-o nondairy product you squirt from a can.

Across from me at my table in the Astor Court was Michael: hands down the handsomest man I knew, or have *ever* known, for that matter. Also, the nicest, the kindest, and probably the wisest.

That day his bright green eyes watched me gaze at the sundae with undisguised delight as the white-coated waiter set it in front of me with tantalizing slowness.

For Michael, a clear glass bowl of melon balls and lemon sherbet. His ability to deny himself the pleasure of a sundae was something my child's brain couldn't wrap itself around.

"Thanks so much," Michael said, adding extreme politeness to his list of enviable qualities.

To which the waiter said—not a word.

The Astor Court was the place to go for a fancy dessert at the St. Regis Hotel. That afternoon it was filled with important-looking people having important-looking conversations. In the background, two symphony-worthy violinists fiddled away as if this were Lincoln Center.

"Okay," Michael said. "Time to play the Jane-and-Michael game."

I clapped my hands together, my eyes lighting up.

Here's how it worked: One of us pointed to a table, and the other had to make up stuff about the people sitting there. The loser paid for dessert.

"Go," he said, pointing. I looked at the three teenage girls dressed in nearly identical pale yellow linen dresses.

Without hesitation, I said, "Debutantes. First season. Just graduated from high school. Maybe in Connecticut. Possibly—probably—Greenwich."

Michael tilted his head back and laughed. "You're definitely spending too much time around adults. Very good, though, Jane. Point for you."

"Okay," I said, gesturing toward another table. "That couple over there. The ones who look like the Cleavers in *Leave It to Beaver*. What's their story?"

The man was wearing a gray-and-blue-checked suit; the woman, a bright pink jacket with a green pleated skirt.

"Husband and wife from North Carolina," Michael rattled off easily. "Wealthy. Own a chain of tobacco shops. He's here on business. She came to do some shopping. Now he's telling her that he wants a divorce."

"Oh," I said, looking down at the table. I let out a deep breath, then took another spoonful of sundae and let the rich flavors unfold in my mouth. "Yeah, I guess everyone gets divorced."

Michael bit his lip. "Oh. Wait, Jane. I got it all wrong. He's *not* asking for a divorce. He's telling her that he has a surprise—he's made arrangements for them to go on a cruise. To Europe on the *QE2*. It's their second honeymoon."

"That's a much better story," I said, smiling. "You get a point. Excellent."

I looked down at my plate and saw that somehow my ice cream sundae had completely vanished. As it always did.

Michael looked around the room dramatically. "Here's one you won't get," he said.

He pointed to a man and a woman just two tables away.

I looked over.

The woman was about forty years old, well dressed, and stunningly pretty. You might have taken her for a movie actress. She wore a bright red designer dress and matching shoes and had a big black pocketbook. Everything about her said, *Look at me!*

The man she was with was younger, pale, and very thin. He was wearing a blue blazer and a patterned silk ascot, which I don't think anyone was wearing even back *then*. He waved his arms enthusiastically as he spoke.

"That's not funny," I said, but I couldn't help grinning and rolling my eyes.

Because, of course, the couple was my mother, Vivienne Margaux, the famous Broadway producer, and that year's celebrity hairdresser, Jason. Jason, the hothouse flower, who didn't have time for a last name.

I looked over at them again. One thing was for sure: My mom *was* beautiful enough to be an actress herself. Once, when I asked her why she hadn't become one, she said, "Honey, I don't want to *ride* the train. I want to *drive* the train."

Every Sunday afternoon when Michael and I had dessert at the St. Regis, my mother and a friend had dessert and coffee there too. That way she could gossip or complain or conduct business but still keep an eye on me, without actually having to be *with* me.

After the St. Regis, we would cap off our Sundays at Tiffany's. My mother loved diamonds, wore them everywhere, collected them the way other people collect crystal unicorns, or those weird ceramic Japanese cats with the one paw in the air.

Of course I was okay, those Sundays, because I had Michael for company. Michael, who was my best friend in the world, maybe my only friend, when I was eight years old.

My imaginary friend.

Two

I SNUGGLED CLOSER to Michael at our table. "Want to know something?" I asked. "It's kind of a bummer."

"What?" he asked.

"I think I know what my mother and Jason are talking about. It's Howard. I think Vivienne's tired of him. Out with the old, in with the new."

Howard was my stepfather, my mother's *third* husband. The third one I knew about, anyway.

Her first husband had been a tennis pro from Palm Beach. He'd lasted only a year.

Then had come Kenneth, my father. He'd done better than the tennis pro, lasting three years. He was really sweet, and I loved him, but he traveled a lot for business. Sometimes I felt as if he forgot about me. I'd heard my mother tell Jason that he'd been "spineless." She didn't know I'd overheard.

She'd said, "He was a good-looking jellyfish of a man who will never amount to anything."

Howard had been around for two years now. He never traveled on business and didn't seem to have a job, other than helping Vivienne. He massaged her feet when she was tired, checked that her food was salt-free, and made sure that our car and driver were absolutely always on time.

"Why do you think that?" Michael asked.

"Little things," I said. "Like Vivienne used to buy him stuff all the time. Fancy loafers from Paul Stuart and ties from Bergdorf Goodman's. But she hasn't given him anything in ages. And, last night, she ate at home. Alone. With me. Howard wasn't even there."

"Where was he?" Michael asked. I could see the sympathy and concern in his eyes.

"I don't know. When I asked Vivienne, she just said, 'Who knows and who cares?'" I imitated my mother's voice, then shook my head. "Okay," I said. "New topic. Guess what day Tuesday is."

Michael tapped his chin a few times. "No idea."

"C'mon. You know perfectly well. You *know*, Michael. This isn't funny."

"Valentine's Day?"

"Stop it!" I told him, kicking him gently under the table. He grinned. "You know what Tuesday is. You have to. It's my birthday!"

"Oh, yeah. Wow, you're getting *old,* Jane."

I nodded. "I think my mother is having a party for me."

"Hmm," Michael said.

"Well, anyway, I don't care about a party, really. What I really want is a real, live puppy."

Michael nodded.

"Cat got your—" I started to say but then stopped in midsentence.

Out of the corner of my eye, I saw Vivienne signing the check. In a minute she and Jason would be standing over our table, hustling me off. This Sunday at the St. Regis was coming to a close. It had been another wonderful afternoon for me and Michael.

"Here she comes, Michael," I whispered. "Look invisible."

Three

VIVIENNE STRODE TOWARD our table as if she owned the St. Regis. Jason trailed along behind her. No one in the Astor Court would have believed that this beautiful woman with the perfect makeup, the perfect skin, the perfect tan, was in any way related to the pudgy eight-year-old with frizzy hair and smudges of fudge sauce on both cheeks.

But there we were. Mother and daughter.

Vivienne kissed me on the cheek and then got down to business. The business of me.

"Jane-Sweetie…" She almost always called me "Jane-Sweetie," as if that were my actual name. "Must you always order two desserts?"

Jason the celebrity hairdresser tried to help. "Well, Vivienne, the second dessert was melon. That's not too bad. Carbs, of course, but—"

"Jane-Sweetie, we've talked about your weight—" my mother began.

"I'm only eight years old," I said. "How about I promise to be anorexic later?"

Michael laughed so hard he nearly fell off his chair.

Even Jason smiled.

Vivienne didn't move a facial muscle. She was always trying not to frown because she didn't want to get wrinkles before her time. Say, ninety or so.

"Don't be precocious with me, Jane-Sweetie." She turned to Jason. "She reads far too many books."

Yeah, I'm terrible that way, I thought. Vivienne turned back to me. "We'll discuss your eating habits at home. In private."

"Anyway," I told her, "that melon isn't even mine. Michael ordered it."

"Ah, yes," said Vivienne, sounding bored, "Michael, the amazing, ever-present imaginary friend." She addressed the chair next to mine, which was empty. Michael was on my other side. "Hello, Michael. How are you today?"

"Hello, Vivienne," said Michael, knowing she couldn't see or hear him. "I'm just peachy, thanks."

All of a sudden I felt Jason tugging at a handful of my hair.

"Hey!" I protested.

"Something must be done about this," he said. "Vivienne, give me one hour with this hair. There's no reason why anyone should walk around like this. She'll come out looking like a *Vogue* model."

"That's great," Michael said. "Just what the world needs—an eight-year-old who looks like a *Vogue* model."

I winced and pulled my hair away from Jason.

"Come, Jane-Sweetie," said Vivienne. "There's a full-cast rehearsal tonight, and I must look in on it." Her latest huge Broadway musical, *The Problem with Kansas,* was opening in days.

"But first we can drop by Tiffany's, like we always do, dear. Our time together."

"What about Jane's hair?" Jason demanded. "When can I schedule her makeover?"

Michael shook his head. "You're perfect the way you are, Jane. You don't need a makeover. Never forget that."

"I won't," I said.

"You won't what?" asked Vivienne. She took a napkin, dipped it in my water glass, and wiped the fudge sauce from my cheeks. "A makeover's a great idea, Jane-Sweetie. There might be a big fancy party in your future."

She remembered! A birthday party! I thought, and suddenly I forgave her for everything else.

"Come along now. I hear Tiffany's calling." Vivienne spun on her four-inch heels and headed for the exit, Jason close behind her.

Michael and I both got up. He leaned down and kissed the top of my head, right on the frizzy hair that pained Jason so.

"See you tomorrow," he said. "Miss you already."

"Miss you already, too."

I looked ahead and saw my mother's slim, tan legs disappearing into the St. Regis's revolving door. She glanced back. "Jane-Sweetie, come! Tiffany's."

I ran to catch up.

I was always doing that.

Four

POOR, POOR, POOR JANE! *Poor, poor little girl!*
The next morning, Michael waited outside Jane's fancy
Park Avenue building, as he always did. It was a good
thing he was invisible: his wrinkled corduroys, faded
yellow golf shirt, and docksiders wouldn't cut it in
this pricey neighborhood.

He was thinking about something pretty amazing that Jane had said when she was only four years
old. Vivienne had been heading off to Europe for a
month. He'd been concerned about how Jane would
cope. But Jane had shrugged it off and said, "Love
means you can never be apart." Michael knew he
would never forget that—out of a four-year-old's
mouth and brain, no less. But that was Jane, wasn't
it? She was an incredible girl.

So what was he going to do with himself on this
lovely day while Jane was locked away in school?

Maybe a big breakfast over at the Olympia Diner—pancakes, sausage, eggs, keep the buttered rye toast coming. He might even get together with a couple of other imaginary friends who worked in the neighborhood. *What exactly were the duties of an imaginary friend?* Pretty much just to make it easier for the child to fit into the world without feeling too alone or scared. *Hours?* Whatever it took. *Benefits?* The incredibly pure love between a kid and an imaginary friend. It didn't get better than that. *Where did he fit in the great cosmic plan?* Well, no one had ever told him.

Michael looked at his watch, an ancient Timex that kept on ticking just as the ads promised it would. It was exactly 8:29. Jane would be down at 8:30, just like every other weekday morning. Jane never kept anyone waiting. Such a sweetheart.

Then he saw her, but pretended not to, as always.

"Gotcha!" she said, wrapping her arms around his waist.

"Whoa!" Michael said. "You're sneakier than a pickpocket in *Oliver Twist.*"

Jane grinned, her smile lighting up the little face that he couldn't get enough of. She hitched her schoolbag onto her small shoulder, and they headed off to school.

"I didn't exactly sneak up," she said. "You were lost somewhere interesting in your thoughts." Jane had a cute way of talking out of the side of her mouth when she was with him, so people didn't think she was loony. Sometimes he let people see him; sometimes he didn't. She could never be sure which—or why. "Life is a mystery," he would say.

As soon as they were out of the doorman's sight, she took his hand. Michael loved that more than he could ever say. It made him feel like—he didn't know. A dad?

"What did Raoul pack for your lunch?" he asked. "Wait—let me guess. Squirrel on whole wheat, wilted iceberg lettuce, hold the three-day-old mayo?"

Jane tugged on his hand. "You're goofy," she said.

"Nah, I'm Sneezy."

"More like Dopey." Jane laughed.

A couple of minutes later—too soon—they were at the tall, imposing school gates, only a block and a half from Jane's apartment building. The entrance was a sea of little girls in navy jumpers over simple white blouses. They all wore either Mary Janes or saddle shoes, socks turned down just so.

"Tomorrow's the special day," Jane said, looking down at her shoes so her classmates wouldn't see her talking to an imaginary friend. "I just might get my puppy. I don't even care what kind anymore. Maybe he'll be at my party. First we have to see *The Problem with Kansas,* though. And you're invited, of course."

The school bell sounded.

"Great. I can't wait to see *Kansas*. You go in now, and I'll be back at three to pick you up. As per usual."

"Okay," she said. "We can talk about what we're going to wear tomorrow night."

"Yeah, you can help pick out some fancy clothes for me. So I don't embarrass you."

Jane's eyes met his squarely. For a split second he had an idea of exactly what she would look like as a grown-up—the serious face, her warm smile, those intelligent eyes that reached right into his soul.

"You could *never* embarrass me, Michael."

She let go of his hand then and ran toward the school building. Michael didn't blink until he saw her head of blond curls slip behind the door. He waited. Jane peeked out again, as she always did. She waved, smiled, then disappeared for good.

Suddenly Michael *needed* to blink. Several times, actually. He felt as if a giant had stepped on his chest. His heart actually hurt.

How was he going to tell Jane that he had to leave her tomorrow?

That was another *duty* of an imaginary friend, and possibly the worst.

Five

I WILL NEVER FORGET that day, in the same way that someone who survived the *Titanic* can't just put it out of her pretty little head. People always remember the worst day of their lives. It becomes part of them forever. So I remember my ninth birthday with piercing clarity.

That day after school, Michael and I got ready. Then we went to the theater and sat in our VIP seats for the opening of *The Problem with Kansas.* I hadn't seen Vivienne all day, so she hadn't had a chance to wish me a happy birthday yet. But Michael had met me at school with flowers. I remember how grown-up that made me feel. Those apricot roses were the most beautiful things I'd ever seen.

I hardly remember the play, but I know that the audience laughed and cried and gasped in all the right places. Michael and I held hands, and I had a fluttering excitement inside my chest. Everything good was about to happen: It was my turn. A birthday party, hopefully a puppy, Michael was with me, my mother would be happy about the play. Everything seemed wonderful, everything seemed possible.

At the curtain call, Vivienne walked onstage with the cast. She pretended to be shy and shocked that everyone liked her new show so much. She bowed, and the audience stood and clapped. I stood up too, and clapped the hardest, and I loved her so much I could hardly bear it. Someday she would love me back just as much, I was sure of it.

Then it was time for my birthday party at our apartment. *Finally!*

The first people to arrive were the dancers from my mother's play. I could have predicted that. Dancers don't make that much money, and they were probably starving after dancing so much. In the front hallway with the black-and-white marble floor, a group of them were taking off their coats, revealing stick-figure bodies. Even at nine years old, I knew I'd never look like that.

"You must be Vivienne's daughter," one of them said. "Jill, right?"

"Jane," I said, but smiled to show I wasn't a total brat.

"I didn't know Vivienne had a kid," one of the other stick figures said. "Hello, Jane. You're cute as a button."

A flock of gazelles, they moved into the huge living room, leaving me to wonder if I'd ever seen a button that qualified as cute.

"Holy Stephen Sondheim!" one dancer said. "I knew Vivienne was rich, but this place is bigger than the Broadhurst Theatre."

By the time I turned around again, it seemed as though there were a hundred people in the room. I searched for Michael and finally saw him standing near the piano player.

The room was as noisy as a theater during intermission. You could barely hear the piano over the chatter. Near the door to the library I saw that Vivienne had arrived, and she was talking to a tall, silver-haired man wearing a tuxedo jacket and blue jeans. I'd seen him at a couple of rehearsals for *Kansas* and knew he was some kind of writer. They were standing very close to each other, and I got a sinking feeling that he was auditioning for the role of Vivienne's fourth husband. Ugh.

A little old lady who played the grandmother in *The Problem with Kansas* hooked me with the handle of her cane.

"You look like a nice girl," she said.

"Thank you. I try to be," I told her. "Can I help you with something?"

"I was wondering if you could go to that wet bar over there and get me a Jack Daniel's and water," she said.

"Sure. Straight up or on the rocks?"

"My goodness. You *are* a sophisticated one. Could you possibly be a midget?"

I laughed and glanced at Michael. He was whispering something to the piano player. What was he up to?

As I began to walk toward one of the bars, I heard a loud voice. "May I have your attention, please?" It was the piano player, and the crowd quieted down immediately.

"I've been told . . . and I'm not sure by whom . . . that this is a very special day for someone. . . . She's nine years old today . . . Vivienne's daughter."

Vivienne's daughter. That's who I was.

I smiled, feeling happy and self-conscious at the same time. Everyone's eyes turned toward me. The leading man from the show picked me up and stood me on a chair, and suddenly I was taller than everyone in the room. I looked for my mother, hoping she was smiling proudly, but I didn't see her anywhere. The writer was gone too. Then music began, and everyone sang "Happy Birthday." There's nothing like having a professional Broadway chorus sing you "Happy Birthday." I think it was the most beautiful "Happy Birthday" I've ever heard. A shiver went right through me, and it probably would have been the happiest moment of my life if my mother had been there to share it with me.

When it was over, the very nice actor put me down, everyone applauded, and the party went back to being an opening night party. The birthday part was over.

Then I heard a familiar voice call my name. "Jane! I think I know this big, beautiful girl." I whirled to see my father, Kenneth. He seemed awfully tall and straight for someone who was supposed to be "spineless."

"Daddy!" I shouted, and ran into his arms.

Six

GOD, DID I LOVE being hugged. Especially by my dad. He wrapped his arms around me, and I could smell cold air and a faint tinge of his after-shave. I breathed in deeply, so happy and relieved he had come.

"You didn't think I'd forget your ninth birthday?" my father asked. He pulled away from me and tugged on my hand. "Okay, quick, out into the front hall. If your mother finds out that I've crashed her party, she'll flip."

"There'll be people to catch her if she does," I said. "But I'm not even sure that she's still here."

We pushed through the crowd, me holding my dad's hand, and in the front hall were two surprises: a big box with a yellow ribbon—and my father's current girlfriend. I remembered Vivienne saying something about Ellie's chest, and how it wasn't real, but I had no idea what she was talking about.

"You remember Ellie, don't you, Jane?" Dad asked.

"Uh-huh. Hi, Ellie. I'm glad you could come." Years of etiquette classes were paying off.

"Happy birthday, Jane," she said. Ellie was very blond and pretty, and she seemed much younger than my mother. I knew Vivienne called Ellie "the schoolgirl" whenever her name was mentioned.

"Open your gift," my dad said. "Ellie helped pick it out."

I pulled on the yellow ribbon, and it came undone immediately. Inside was a lot of tissue paper, and I excitedly clawed my way through it. My fingers touched something soft and velvety—but not alive. I reached in and pulled out the biggest, *purplest* stuffed poodle I'd ever seen. It had a poufy topknot on its head, a rhinestone collar, and a heart-shaped gold tag that said "Gigi."

Pretty much the total opposite of the puppy I had wanted.

"Thanks, Daddy," I said, putting a big smile on my face. "This is so fun!" I tried to push all thoughts of a real, warm, wiggling puppy that would be mine, all mine, from my mind. *No real puppy...stuffed purple poodle instead.*

"Thank Ellie, too," Daddy said.

"Thank you, Ellie," I said politely, and she leaned down and kissed me. I recognized her perfume: Chanel No. 5. My father used to give it to my mother. I wondered if Ellie knew.

"Okay," Dad said, standing up. "Now we're off to Nantucket."

I felt my heart jump. *"We are?"* I almost screamed.

Ellie and my father looked at each other awkwardly.

"No, honey," said my dad. "I meant that Ellie and I are off to Nantucket. Your mother would kill me if I took you away from your birthday party."

Yeah, I'm sure she would notice, I thought bleakly. "I understand," I said, trying hard not to cry on the spot. "It's just that I love Nantucket. I really, really love Nantucket. And so does Michael."

"We'll go there again, Jane. I promise," my father said. "And your friend Michael can come, too."

I'm sure he meant it, because my father never said anything he didn't mean. But it made me so sad to see him help Ellie on with her coat.

"You going to be okay?" Ellie asked. Actually, I liked her. She was always very kind to me. I hoped my father would marry her soon. He needed hugs, too. Everybody does. Maybe even Vivienne did.

"Of course. It's my birthday. Who's not okay on their birthday?"

We hugged one another. We kissed one another. We said good-bye, and then my father and Ellie got into the elevator and were gone into the night, on their merry way to Nantucket.

The opening night party was in full swing. It was as if no one had even sung "Happy Birthday" just a few minutes ago. There was no point in me staying.

I wove through the crowd of grown-ups and finally ran down the long, thickly carpeted, silent corridor that led to my bedroom. I slammed the door behind me and flung myself on my bed, burying my face in my pillow. Here, with no one to see me, I started to weep like the world's biggest crybaby.

Then the door opened.

It was Michael. Thank goodness, it was Michael, come to save me.

Seven

JANE WAS SOBBING on her bed all by herself when he came in. She sure didn't look like a birthday girl. But then, why would she, poor kid?

Michael sighed, then sat down beside her and wrapped his arms around the little girl who didn't deserve to be hurt like this. No child did.

"It's okay, honey. Let it all out," he whispered against her hair, which always smelled of Johnson and Johnson's Baby Shampoo. It was now one of his favorite scents.

"Okay. But you asked for it."

Snuffling, her small face streaked with tears, Jane pulled off her shoes and dropped them on the floor.

"I think Vivienne totally forgot my birthday," she said, and she shuddered with leftover tears. "And my dad came, which was good, but then he left in about two minutes. And he was going to Nantucket, my favorite place in the world! Without me! And I didn't get a puppy, either."

Jane held the purple poodle against her cheek. He had noticed that she often cuddled objects close to her—a winter coat, a pillow, a stuffed animal. She had a lot of hugs to give, but not enough people to give them to.

"You're a good listener," she said, with one last sniffle. "Thanks. I feel better."

Michael looked around her room. It was pure Jane: stacks of chapter books written for much older kids. A real saxophone in the corner. A large poster with vocabulary words—in French. Over her desk, an autographed picture of Warren Beatty. Vivienne had brought it back from a three-month business trip to Los Angeles, during which she hadn't come home once to see her daughter.

Now Michael had to talk to Jane. The place—her cozy room, away from that stupid party—couldn't have been better. The timing—right after she'd been hurt by both of her parents on her birthday—couldn't have been worse.

"You are an amazing, amazing girl," Michael said. "Do you know that? You must."

"Sort of, but only because you tell me every other day," she said with a watery smile.

"You're beautiful, inside and out," he went on. "You're incredibly smart. Well-read. Funny. Considerate. And generous. You've got so much to give."

Suddenly Jane looked very alert. He had just said she was *smart*—and she was about to prove it to him, wasn't she?

"Michael, what are you trying to say? What's going on? Something bad."

His legs weakened and his eyesight blurred. *Why now? Why Jane? Why him?*

"You're nine now," he forced himself to say. "You're a big girl. And so...and so—I'm leaving you tonight, Jane. I have to go."

"I know you do. But you'll be back tomorrow. Like always."

Michael swallowed. This was impossible. It was breaking his heart.

"No, Jane. The thing is, I'll never be back again. I don't have a choice in this. It's a rule." Just saying the words made him feel worse than he ever had. Jane was special. She was different. He didn't know why, he just knew she was. For the first time, the rule about when to leave a child struck Michael as stupid and unfair. He would have rather died than cause Jane this much pain. But it was true that he had no choice. He never had.

She didn't cry, didn't move a muscle in her face—

just like Vivienne. She looked Michael squarely in the eyes and said absolutely nothing. There was an awful stillness about her that he'd never seen.

"Jane, did you hear me?" he finally had to ask.

There was a pause that seemed to go on forever.

"I'm not ready for you to go," she said, and large tears started to roll down her cheeks again. "I'm really not ready."

When she grabbed a tissue to wipe her nose, he saw that her small hands were shaking. And *that* just killed him. Those delicate little hands trembling uncontrollably. It was unbearable.

Damn it, he thought. Then an idea came to him, but this was something he'd never done before, not with any other child.

"Jane, I'll tell you a secret. It's a secret I've never told anyone, and you can't ever tell anyone either. *It's the secret of imaginary friends.*"

"I don't want to hear your secrets," she said, her voice wavering, but Michael kept going.

"Children have imaginary friends to help guide them into their lives. We help children feel less alone, help them find their place in the world, in their families. But then we have to leave, *have to*. It's always been that way, and it will always be that way, Jane. That's just... how it works."

"But I told you, *I'm not ready*."

Michael let her in on another secret. "Once I leave, you won't even remember me, sweetheart. No one ever does. If you ever think of me, I'll just seem like a dream." It was the one thing that made any of this acceptable at all.

Jane grabbed his arm and held on tightly. "Please don't leave me, Michael. I'm begging you. You can't—not now, not ever! You don't know how important you are to me!"

"You'll see, Jane," he promised her. "You'll forget me, and it won't hurt tomorrow. Besides, you said it yourself: Love means you can never be apart. So we'll never be apart, Jane, because I love you so much. I'll always, always love you."

And with those words, Michael began to fade out of the room, in imaginary friend–style, and as he did he heard sweet little Jane's last words.

"Michael, please don't go! Please don't! If you go, I'll have no one. I'll *never* forget you, Michael, no matter what. I'll never forget you!"

Which brings the story to today.

Not an imaginary today either.

The real one.

PART TWO

Twenty-three Years Older, but Not Necessarily That Much Smarter

Eight

ELSIE MCANN LOOKED as pale as the froth on a latte, panic-stricken, and possibly close to a fatal stroke. So what else was new? After all, Elsie had been the dragonlike receptionist at my mother's production company, ViMar Productions, for twenty-eight long and stressful years, and here she was, still breathing, if not exactly breathing fire anymore.

"Oh, thank God, you're finally here, Jane," she said, relief flooding into her voice.

"It's barely ten o'clock."

"I don't know what's wrong, but Vivienne's been out here a hundred times, asking about you."

"Well, tell her I'm here now."

But Elsie wouldn't have to. I could already hear Vivienne's stiletto heels clicking down the corridor.

"Where have you been, Jane-Sweetie? It's practically

noon," she asked, a split second before she actually came into view.

"It's ten o'clock," I said again.

"And where have you *been?*" she said, then kissed me on the cheek, as she always did. My morning kiss.

Actually, I had been in my apartment, drinking coffee and watching Matt Lauer interview a woman on how to organize an out-of-control garage. (By the way, extensive use of Peg-Boards is the answer.)

I headed down the hall and into my office, with Vivienne following me.

"I hope that paper bag you're carrying does *not* hold a fattening blueberry muffin."

"No, it does not," I answered truthfully. The bag held a fattening maple-walnut doughnut, *glazed.*

I sat down at my desk and began going through a one-inch stack of phone messages. A lot were from agents and therefore *lies.*

One was from my "personal shopper" at Saks, Vivienne's idea. More lies.

Five messages were marked "Your mother."

One was from Hugh McGrath, my boyfriend. The light of my life, the bane of my existence, all wrapped up in one hot, charming package.

The next message was from my dermatologist, returning my call.

The only other significant message was from Karl Friedkin, and it actually *was* important. He was a wealthy real estate developer, *and* he was very interested in investing in my movie project.

Three years ago my mother had allowed me to produce a play, all on my own. It had a cast of two—an eight-year-old girl and a thirty-five-year-old man. It had two sets—the Astor Court of the St. Regis Hotel and a Manhattan apartment. I was pretty sure that Vivienne had thought it would be so cheap to produce that when it flopped it wouldn't be a huge loss.

The play was called *Thank Heaven,* and it was based not at all loosely on my long-ago relationship with Michael, my imaginary friend. Maybe producing this play had been my way of trying not to forget Michael. Maybe it was just an adorable idea for a play.

To both Vivienne's and my astonishment, *Thank Heaven* had been a hit. A smash hit, actually, and a Tony winner. Audiences had loved the story of the chubby little girl and her handsome imaginary friend. When Michael finally left her, you could hear the audience sobbing. Often enough, I had been one of them.

A blowup of a quote from Ben Browning in the *New York Times* hung over my desk:

CALL ME A SENTIMENTAL FOOL, OR MUCH
WORSE IF YOU LIKE, BUT "THANK HEAVEN" IS
IRRESISTIBLE. LIKE LIFE AT ITS BEST, IT IS THE
PERFECT COMBINATION OF CHARM, TEARS,
AND LAUGHTER.

Of course, *Thank Heaven* wouldn't bring Michael
back, but it had brought Hugh McGrath into my life.
Hugh had played Michael, and then he became my
real-life boyfriend.

When I'd told Vivienne that I wanted to produce
a movie of *Thank Heaven,* she'd said, "That's not
a terrible idea, but you'll never be able to do it on
your own, Jane-Sweetie. You'll definitely need my
help. Fortunately for you, I don't have too much on
my plate right now."

The plan was to raise half the production money
ourselves, then ask a Hollywood studio for the rest.
Vivienne had said she'd match whatever Karl Friedkin came up with.

"I'm breaking the cardinal rule of production.
Never invest your own money," Vivienne had said.
"But, after all, you're family, Jane-Sweetie."

Ah, she remembered.

Nine

IN MY OFFICE, Vivienne said, "Call Karl Friedkin. Right now. This minute! Your mother commands it." She was only half joking.

Faithful servant that I am, I pressed his number on speed dial.

"Wait a second, Jane-Sweetie. Hold on. Hang up. Let me think."

I hung up.

Vivienne tented her fingers together as she paced around my small office. It almost looked as if she were praying to the patron saint of theater backers. "Here's what I want you to let Karl know," she said. "Tell him there's a great deal of interest in the project from Gerry Schwartz at Phoenix Films, and Gerry has an eye for big hits."

"Oh my God!" I said. "When did Phoenix call?"

She gave me an exasperated look. "Oh, for God's

sake, Jane-Sweetie. They didn't. But let Friedkin think they're interested." She went on: "Tell him that if he doesn't kick in the money today, well, tomorrow's going to be too late."

I put down the phone. "Mother, I can see stretching the truth. But outright lying? You know I hate that."

Another exasperated look. "It's how the game is played."

"By the way, how did you know Karl Friedkin called me?" I asked suspiciously.

"A mother's intuition," she said, click-clacking toward the door.

"You went through my phone messages."

She pretended to be shocked. "I would never do such a thing." Looking affronted, she swept out the door, only to sweep back in a second later.

"Oh, and after you call Karl Friedkin and get our money, don't forget to call your dermatologist back."

Ten

MY BOYFRIEND, Hugh McGrath, was ridiculously handsome, but should that be held against him? Okay, well, maybe. I can think of a few reasons. Once, on a beach in East Hampton, a man had walked up to him and said, "Where can I buy a smile like that?" And he'd been serious. That was the kind of guy Hugh was. The kind that something like that would happen to. The kind of guy with velvety brown eyes, a perfect nose, high cheekbones, and a chiseled chin worthy of Bond, James Bond.

Hugh was a Broadway actor, nominated for a Tony when he was nineteen. He'd been born with the gift of gab and an innate ability to sell ice to polar bears. Once he'd leaned on his elbow in bed and told me that just the sight of me in the morning made him deliriously happy. Since I know what

I look like when I wake up, my response was "You want mustard with that baloney?"

Tonight he was meeting me for dinner at Babbo, our favorite Italian restaurant in Greenwich Village. Twenty-some years ago, when I was a little girl, Babbo had been called the Coach House. My mother and I would go there sometimes on Sunday nights. I would always order the black bean soup, and she would always say, "No sour cream in the soup, Jane-Sweetie. Remember, you had a huge ice cream sundae a few hours ago." Yes, *with Michael.*

Tonight I arrived at the restaurant before Hugh, and the stunning Russian-born blonde at the reservation desk led me upstairs to the dining loft. Once I was seated, I couldn't help people-watching. I'll admit it, I'm an addict from way back.

Across the aisle from me was an eye-catching couple, a black woman and a blond white guy, both in their twenties. His navy blue Ralph Lauren suit said "successful attorney." Her long legs said "runway model." They were clearly in love, crazy about each other. For tonight, anyway.

At the next table was another couple in their mid-to-late forties. She wore a pair of jeans and your basic five-hundred-dollar T-shirt. He wore chinos, a dark brown shirt, a darker brown suede jacket. His eyeglasses were authentic 1950s black. I decided they were art dealers, and she was an artist. It was their second anniversary. She was trying to get him to taste her black fettuccine with squid.

Yes, I was playing the Jane-and-Michael game. And, yes, I didn't even realize it. And, yes, damn it, Hugh was fifteen minutes late for our date. It wasn't the first time, especially in the last few weeks. Well, actually, ever since I'd been going out with him.

Eleven

I TOOK OUT my cell phone and placed it on the table. I ordered a Bellini, delicious, perfect, and sipped it while I waited for my date to arrive.

Hugh was now a half hour late. *Damn him.*

Then I realized this was the third time in a row that Hugh had been really late without a phone call. I tried to work up concern, like maybe he'd gotten hit by a taxi, maybe he was in the hospital, maybe he'd gotten mugged, but quickly shut it down when I realized it was my anger talking.

Hugh was probably at the gym. He was obsessed with staying in ridiculously good shape, and how could I object to that?

MAYBE BECAUSE HUGII was now cxactly one hour late. Nobody needs to be in such good shape.

A second Bellini had made me a little light-headed and hungry.

"Perhaps I could bring a little antipasto for you, Miss Margaux?" the waiter asked. He was one of my favorites, always so nice, and he remembered me every time. Well, I'd been coming here for years.

"You know, I think I'll order."

I REMEMBER being hungry—and then I remember being full. I remember looking down and seeing my hand, holding a spoon with some elaborate chocolate pudding kind of thing on it. I remember the waiter placing a small cup of espresso and a plate of biscotti on the table.

"I've put the check on Ms. Margaux's tab," the waiter said. "It was so nice to see you again. I hope you enjoyed your meal."

"Everything was wonderful." *Maybe not everything.*

I walked out of the restaurant into a chilly spring night in Manhattan. Alone. My cheeks were burning, but whether it was the Bellinis or the humiliation, I couldn't tell. I was living that old cliché: When your own romantic life is falling apart, everyone else's looks fabulous. Did I really need to see a middle-aged couple chatting quietly and holding hands in the park? Or the teenagers who decided to stop and kiss eagerly just a few feet away from where I was walking? No. I did not. Why was everyone in New York City suddenly madly in love while I was walking alone with my arms folded across my chest?

My cell phone rang.

Hugh! Of course it was Hugh. And his excuse for tonight would be... what?

"Hello?" A little too breathless, maybe? Too Bellinified?

"Jane Margaux?" the voice on the line said.

"This is Jane," I answered, not recognizing whoever it was.

"This is Verizon Wireless, and we'd like to tell you about our exciting new calling plan."

I flipped the phone closed and dropped it back into my bag. I wished I was the kind of person who was reckless enough to throw it into the nearest trash can. Of course, if I did, I'd only have to fish it out again, and of course someone I knew would be walking by right at that moment, when I was pawing through the trash, and then this day would be complete.

I swallowed hard and felt hot tears behind my eyes. *Perfect. Crying on the street. A new low, even for me.*

I was a pathetic loser. The sooner I faced it, the

better. The facts were that I was on the wrong side of thirty, I worked for my *mother,* and I was the kind of woman whose gorgeous, too-good-for-her boyfriend stood her up at their favorite restaurant, and that was the way it was.

Twelve

MICHAEL WAS POLISHING OFF his second hot dog, savoring every juicy bite, every burst of flavor in his mouth. *Man, was he ever hungry! Starved! Ravenous! And thank God, he didn't have to worry about what he ate.*

Here he was, between assignments, back in New York, killing time. He was hanging out, having some fun, waiting to hear what was up next for him. He'd seen just about every movie released, gone to the best museums (like the Museum of the American Indian), plus visited most of the doughnut and coffee joints on the island of Manhattan in single-minded pursuit of the best old-fashioned cake doughnut known to man. And, oh yeah, he was taking boxing lessons.

Yes, boxing lessons. Over the years he'd discovered so many activities that he loved, a lot of which he'd thought he wouldn't like at all. Such as boxing. But it was terrific exercise, and it really built up the self-confidence. Self-awareness, too. Also, it brought him closer to people, in a weird sort of way. Sometimes a little too close.

Two nights a week, in a seedy second-floor gym on 8th Street, an old black guy with whiskey and peppermint on his breath taught him how to throw reasonably crisp punches, how to guard himself against attack, how to get in close and slam left hooks into the body of an opponent.

He'd pretty much gotten used to eighteen-year-old black and Hispanic kids banging his nose till blood oozed out. And being called "old man" by his sparring partners, who seemed to like him anyway. Hell, everybody liked Michael. That was his job, right?

But he still wasn't used to the wicked appetite he had after every workout. The post-workout hunger was so fierce it could be satisfied only by three or four hot dogs and at least two chocolate Yoo-Hoos from a Manhattan pushcart.

Tonight he'd ordered his hot dogs and Yoo-Hoos and was thinking how nice it was to be back in New York. He'd just finished a Seattle assignment with a six-year-old boy whose parents were lesbians. The problem had been that the two women were way too involved with little Sam. He took too many music lessons and too many acro classes, had too many tutors, and heard the question *"And how do you feel about that, Sam?"* much too frequently.

Michael's "Polite Assertiveness Training Lessons" were put into action, and the two moms had ended up actually liking Sam's feisty new behavior. Michael had helped Sam to be who Sam was. Then, of course, he'd had to leave the boy, and Sam no longer remembered him. But that was how it worked, and Michael had no control over it.

Now Michael was sort of on vacation, enjoying himself, looking at girls, bicycling in Central Park, eating whatever he wanted. He did whatever the hell he felt like doing, ate what he wanted and never put on an ounce, and got his brains bashed in twice a week. How could you beat that?

As he took the last slug of his second Yoo-Hoo, a woman passed by, and his eyes automatically followed her, appreciating her curves. Nothing new there. He was always noticing women in New York. He fancied that she looked as if she were trying to be brave, to make the best of it, and he smiled, suddenly remembering the way little Jane Margaux...

But then...

A certain tilt of her head...

The walk...kind of "breezy."

That was weird, but, nah...It couldn't be.

But the swing of her arms...

Well, maybe...*A glance his way. Those eyes. No, not those eyes!*

It was her! Had to be. But there was no way.

Was there? Could it be?

Her hair wasn't as curly as it was when she was a kid, but it was still blond. She wore a loose black coat and carried a big leather bag—half briefcase, half pocketbook.

Michael's jaw dropped. It was completely impossible, but it had to be Jane!

Oh God, it was his Jane Margaux! She was right there, not fifty feet from him.

Michael lunged away from the cart after her, causing the hot dog vendor to stare at him suspiciously.

This had never happened, Michael marveled. Never, ever, had he run into one of his kids as a grown-up!

Jane was walking slowly, seeming lost in her thoughts. So he walked slowly too, trying to decide what to do next. He was at a loss—for words, ideas, everything.

At the corner of Sixth Avenue and 8th Street, she hailed a cab and got one immediately. She ran a few steps and got in, pulling the door shut after her. Michael hung back. He *knew* what he should do now. *Let her go, file it away under "bizarre coincidences."*

But that wasn't what he did. Instead he flagged down the next taxi speeding along Sixth Avenue. He said something he'd always wanted to: "Follow that cab!"

Follow Jane.

He had to.

Thirteen

THE CABDRIVER OBLIGINGLY stomped on the gas, and Michael's head flew back against the seat. *This was so strange. Why bump into one of his kids, all grown-up? Never happened before. So why now? What did it mean?* Closing his eyes, he said a silent prayer, but, as usual, got no answer. In that way, at least, he figured he was just like everybody else: put here for a reason, but damned if he could figure out what it was. One thing, though: The longer he was here, the more "human" he felt. Was that a clue, that he was becoming more human? And was that a good thing?

After all, what did Michael know about himself? Not as much as he wanted to, for sure. He had a limited memory of the past, was able to recall only fuzzy faces, indistinct periods of time. He had no concrete idea of how long he'd been on the job or

exactly how many kids he'd looked after. He knew
for certain that he loved what he did, except, on
average, maybe one day a month. Also on average,
he would stay with a child for four to six years. Then
he'd have to go, whether he wanted to or not,
whether the kid wanted him to or not. Then there
would be a little break for him, a sabbatical, like the
one he was on now. One day he'd wake up in a different city, and in his mind he would *know* the next
boy or girl, and he would go to them. Otherwise, all
his needs were met. He wasn't exactly human, he
wasn't an angel—he was just a friend. And he was
damn good at it.

Meanwhile, the cab with Jane inside was shooting straight up Sixth Avenue.

It turned right on Central Park South. Michael's
cab followed.

Left again on Park Avenue.

*Was she going to her mother's apartment? Oh,
Jane, no! Don't tell me you're still living with your
mother!* He winced, now sure that following her had
been a terrible idea. He remembered Vivienne Margaux, her huge ego, her larger-than-life personality.
She'd spent Sunday afternoons with Jane, and occasionally kissed her cheek, but that was about it.
Jane's school had been a block and a half from the

apartment, but Vivienne had never once taken Jane there.

Michael groaned when Jane's taxi stopped at 535 Park Avenue—but she didn't get out.

Instead the doorman came up to the cab's rear window, and Jane handed him two large manila envelopes. He seemed happy to see her, giving her a big smile and tipping his hat. Jane smiled back at him, looking less sad. They even slapped five.

Then Jane's cab took off again.

Okay. At least she wasn't still living with Vivienne. Michael's cab followed as Jane's taxi stopped again at 75th and Park. The building's doorman walked up to the cab and opened the car door for her.

Michael quickly handed his driver a twenty-dollar bill, keeping an eye on Jane. She gathered her briefcase and folded her black coat over one arm.

She looked, well, terrific. Very grown-up. Very attractive. So strange, to see little Jane Margaux looking like this. Like a woman. Jane smiled warmly at this doorman, and he smiled back. She was Michael's same old Jane. Kind to everyone, friends with everybody. Always a smile for the world.

Michael stayed behind a huge cement planter, feeling ridiculous, like a kid playing a spy game, but something was compelling him to stay. He heard the doorman say, "Mr. McGrath stopped by. He said if you came home to tell you that he would probably miss dinner tonight."

"Thanks, Martin. He made it to dinner after all," Jane said. But she bit her lip.

The doorman paused, his hand on the heavy glass lobby door. "He didn't, did he, Miss Jane?"

Jane sighed. "No, Martin, he didn't."

"Miss Jane, you know what I think."

"I know, I know. I'm a sap. I'm an idiot."

"No, Miss Jane," the doorman said repressively. "It's Mr. McGrath who's the idiot, if you'll forgive my saying so. You deserve better than him."

From behind the planter, Michael heartily agreed. Jane had been stood up! He was now absolutely positive it was his Jane, from so long ago. He'd have known her voice anywhere. It was more mature, deeper, but recognizable all the same. And after all this time, she was still getting hurt, wasn't she? People were still letting her down, not treating her like the special treasure she was. What was that all about? How could anyone stand to hurt her?

Actually, Michael had been one of those people who had let her down, he acknowledged with shame. He'd hurt her. But he'd had no choice! There had been nothing, zero, zip, that he could do about it!

Anyway, she'd forgotten him the next day. It almost made his hurting her not really count. Not like this schmuck McGrath.

But why had Michael run into her again?

But she had gone into her building now, and suddenly Martin the doorman was by the planter, looking down suspiciously at Michael.

"Can I help you, sir?"

Michael winced and stood up straight. "No—ah, thank you. I doubt it very much. I'll just be on my way."

"Yes, sir. I was thinking the same thing."

Fourteen

MY MOTHER HAD DONE everything but physically throw her body in front of the door to keep me from moving out of her apartment and getting my own place after college.

"Move out? Nonsense! Why on earth would you want to move out? Raoul is here! *I'm* here! Jane-Sweetie, with me and Raoul and the Chinese restaurant on Lexington, you have everything you could possibly want."

Yes, Mother. Everything but privacy, a life, and perhaps my sanity.

"You can't manage without me!" Vivienne had insisted. "Who will help you pick out your clothes? Remind you to stick to your diet? Help with your practically nonexistent love life? Oh, which reminds me. My friend Tori gave me her cousin's number, and I really think you should call him—apparently he's an ear surgeon and very successful. But, Jane-Sweetie..."

So that pretty much convinced me.

As the movers were taking my Biedermeier dresser out the door, Vivienne had admitted a partial—and only a partial—defeat. "We'll try it for a few months, Jane-Sweetie. And when it doesn't work out, you can sublet it and come back."

No matter how much I might come to hate my new digs, I would not be moving back. Not even if I cried myself to sleep in my lonely pillow every night. It would still be *my* pillow in *my* apartment, and no one would be walking in on me to ask which earrings went with what outfit.

Vivienne had then decided to make the best of it, in her own way. When I was away on a two-week business trip, she had completely redecorated my new place. I came back to my private little haven to find that my bedroom and living room were white on white, just like hers. The kitchen, which I used exclusively for reheating take-out food, was equipped like a restaurant: professional stove, warming ovens, two dishwashers, the glass-door Sub-Zero refrigerator with the pretty display lighting. There was a lone container of fat-free yogurt showing through the glass.

I'd been too overwhelmed to undecorate or redecorate the redecoration. But I had managed to add my own touch: a photo of my mother, my father, and me, when I was very small. We were in Greece, standing at the foot of the Parthenon, and we were actually smiling. Had we ever really been that happy as a family, even for that one day? Even for an instant? I liked to believe that we were.

So I'd hung the photograph in the front hall. My mother had spotted it immediately on her next visit. She'd sniffed and said, "If I give you one of my lesser Picasso drawings, would you consider replacing that sentimental trash?"

Every time I came home and looked at that photo, I smiled.

But not tonight.

A little tight from the drinks at Babbo, hurt because of Hugh's continuing thoughtlessness, and guilty about eating too much, I switched on the hallway light and looked at that happy family at the Parthenon. But for some reason, it didn't make me feel any better.

The answering machine in my bedroom told me I had three new messages.

I pressed the Play button. Come on, Hugh. Redeem yourself. Tell me you're in the hospital. Cheer me up.

"Jane-Sweetie. Where on earth are you? Are you there . . . listening? Pick up, darling. Come on, pick up. I just had the most brilliant thought—"

I pressed Erase and moved on to the next message.

"This is a reminder from The Week *magazine. Your complimentary six-month subscription—"*

Erase again.

One last message. It was my old college roommate.

"Jane, it's Colleen. Are you sitting?"

I sat on the edge of my bed and eased my shoes off.

"Okay, here's the rather unexpected news. I'm getting married. After Dwight and I divorced, I thought I would never meet anybody else, or want to. But Ben is great. Honestly. Cross my heart! Wait till you meet him. Never been married, works as a lawyer here in Chicago. The wedding is September twelfth, and you have to be a bridesmaid. I'll try you again tomorrow. Hope everything's going okay with you, too. I love you, Jane. Oh yeah—I'm writing short stories again too. Yippee! Hope you're well."

I was happy for Colleen, I really was. All she'd ever wanted was to write fiction and raise a family, and now she was getting another chance at both. Yippee, indeed. I *was* happy for her. Really. Mostly.

I walked into the bathroom and took off my eye shadow and mascara with those little "non-oily hypo-allergenic" eye pads. I washed my face with Caswell-Massey almond soap. ("If it was good enough for

Jackie Kennedy," my mother had told me, "it's good enough for you.")

Then I climbed into bed and clicked on my laptop. I began making contract notes for my movie. I would forward them to Vivienne's attorney tonight, and then he could draft a formal legal proposal to send to Karl Friedkin.

An hour later, I shut off the computer. I was too tired to think straight and hoped the notes made sense. Getting out of bed, I padded through the quiet apartment. In the kitchen, I poured myself a glass of water that my mother had shipped over from Sweden. I took several virtuous sips, but already my fingers were tingling with longing. I put the water down.

Jane, be strong.

I looked at the cabinet doors, the ones beneath the farmhouse slab sink.

I reached my hand out.

Don't go there, Jane. Don't do this.

I opened the cabinet under the kitchen sink.

You are now officially staring into the abyss. Step away! It's not too late!

I knelt. And since I was getting ready to worship, it was appropriate.

Behind the Brillo pads, behind the Windex, behind the Soft Scrub, I took out my secret box of Oreos.

Written on the box was: "For Emergency Use Only! This Means You!"

I felt that tonight qualified. I ate four Oreos slowly, relishing every bite, every perfect combination of crunchy, chocolatey goodness mixed with sweet, creamy filling.

My ritual complete, I headed back to bed.

With two more Oreos in my hand.

The extra Oreos were gone before I hit the pillow.

Fifteen

MICHAEL'S APARTMENT was in SoHo, one of his favorite parts of New York City, or any city, for that matter. Like everybody else, he had a certain amount of free will, could make most of his own choices. He just had a job to do, a *mission*—to be an imaginary friend to children. It wasn't a bad job, by any means. He sometimes said out loud, "I love my work."

Still, he enjoyed these sabbaticals between assignments, between his kids. There was no telling how long they might last, so he'd learned to make the most of every day, to live in the moment, all that good stuff people liked to talk about, especially on TV, but often weren't very good at putting into action.

That night he got back to his brownstone at about 11:00, totally shaken up about having seen Jane, the grown-up Jane. It had been a huge shock. Jane Margaux. Wow.

By the time Michael had hit the second landing, on the way to his fourth-floor walk-up, he could feel rock music drumming down from above, vibrating through the stairs. No doubt as to where it was coming from: Owen Pulaski's apartment.

Owen Pulaski. Michael wasn't sure what to make of that devil-may-care, happy-go-lucky lug of a man-child. He was certainly friendly enough, outgoing, always made an effort. In fact, as Michael got to the fourth floor, Owen was just greeting a couple of women at the door of his apartment. The women were tall, slender, inhumanly gorgeous, and they were laughing at whatever Owen had just said to them. Owen was about six foot three, burly, with a boyish grin that Michael assumed was hard to resist.

"Mikey, c'mon to my party. Don't insult me now. Don't you dare insult me," Owen called across the hall.

"Thanks, thanks, I'm kind of beat tonight," Michael said, but Owen was already crossing the space between them, and then he had his arm wrapped around Michael.

"This is Claire de Lune, and this is Cindy Two," Owen said, nodding at both stunners. "They're brilliant students at Columbia—I think it's Columbia—

who moonlight as beautiful models. Ladies, this is Michael. He's great. He's a surgeon at New York Hospital."

"I'm not a surgeon anywhere," said Michael as he was dragged into the packed, loud, overheated party at Owen's place.

"Hey, hi," said one of the women, a tall brunette whom Owen had called Claire de Lune. "I'm Claire... *Parker.* Owen is, well, *Owen.*"

Michael turned his wince into something resembling a smile. "Hi, how are you, Claire?"

"Not great, but let's not get into that. We just met, right?"

Michael sensed trouble inside the girl, and he couldn't resist; he'd never met a lonely, depressed soul he didn't want to try to help somehow. Was it his fatal flaw? The way he was made? He had no idea, and he had stopped worrying about things he couldn't control. Well, mostly he had stopped.

"No, it's okay. I'm interested," he said to Claire.

"Sure you are." She laughed. Someone passing by pressed drinks into both of their hands, and she laughed again. "Guys love to hear about our problems, our inner feelings, all that stuff."

"No, I do, actually. Let's talk."

So Michael listened to Claire Parker's life story for well over an hour in a tiny corner of the hallway leading to the kitchen. She was conflicted about wanting to be a teacher, which she was in school for, and all the money she was suddenly making as a model with the Ford Agency.

Finally she looked into his eyes, smiled very sweetly, and said, "Michael, even though you're not a surgeon, and I'm not Claire de Lune, do you want to come home with me? My roommate is on a shoot in London, and my cat isn't the jealous type. You up for it? Say yes."

Sixteen

TO BE HONEST, candid, *whatever*, it wouldn't have been the first time something like this had happened to Michael, mostly on his sabbaticals, but sometimes during work stints as well. After all, he was able to make choices, he had a life, and he wasn't impervious to beauty.

What he said to Claire was "Actually, I live right across the hall."

Michael's place was a sublet, fairly tidy and nicely furnished, the apartment of an anthropology professor at NYU who was in Turkey for the semester. Michael had a knack for finding great apartments, another perk of the job.

"Your turn to talk," Claire said, curling up on the sofa. She tucked her long legs under her and didn't pull her skirt down to cover her knees. She patted the cushion next to her. "Come. Sit. Tell me everything." Michael sat, and Claire traced one finger down his cheek. "Who is she? What happened? Why are you available? Are you?"

Michael laughed, mostly at himself. "Funny you should ask. There *was* someone, sort of. I lost track of her for a long time. And then tonight, I think I found her again. Sort of. It's kind of complicated."

"It always is." Claire grinned. "I *am* interested, and we have all night. You have whiskey? Spirits of some kind?"

In point of fact, Michael did (at least the professor did), very nice wine, which he would replace before he left. He opened a bottle of Caymus, then a second bottle—ZD—as he and the lovely Claire de Lune talked and talked until 4:00 in the morning, at which point they finally fell asleep in each other's arms, in their clothes. And that was all right. Perfect, actually.

In the morning, gentleman that he was, Michael made Claire a breakfast of whole wheat toast, eggs, and coffee. He prided himself on his coffee. This week it was shade-grown Kona. When she was leaving, she turned and draped one arm around Michael's shoulders. "Thank you, Michael. I had a wonderful time." She leaned in—they were almost the same height—and kissed Michael on the lips. "She's a lucky girl."

"Who?" asked Michael, not understanding.

"Jane. The one you were talking about last night, during the second bottle of wine." Claire gave him a resigned little smile. "Good luck with her."

Seventeen

AT 7:15 AM, I, the boss's daughter, was the very first one in at ViMar Productions (with the exception of the mail boy, a tap-dancing British teenager, who I think was actually living under the sorting table in the mail room).

It was 4:00 in the morning in Los Angeles, so I could send only e-mail and voicemail there. But it was noon in London, and that meant I could connect with Carla Crawley, the production head of the London company of *Thank Heaven*. The play was an even bigger hit in London than it had been in New York. The sets, the actors, everything was better quality over there.

"Jane, I'm so glad you called. We're having a slight problem. Seems that Jeffrey doesn't like the new girl we've cast."

Jeffrey was Jeffrey Anderson, the British heart-throb who was playing Michael.

"Jeffrey says he doesn't relate as well to this new little girl. But believe me, Jane, the girl is brilliant, a real heart-tugger. Best of all, she's eleven years old, but looks eight, so she can *talk*."

"Look, call Jeffrey's agent and suggest they reread the part in his contract that says he has to play opposite a three-legged monkey if we want him to."

"I'll pass the word along, *Vivienne Junior*," Carla Crawley said, chuckling. A shudder shot down my spine. *Vivienne Junior. Oh God, say it isn't so.*

Eighteen

AT 9:00 SHARP, my personal assistant, Mary-Louise, showed up at the office. MaryLouise: totally honest, totally sarcastic, with the toughest, thickest Bronx accent this side of the Throgs Neck Bridge.

"Morning, Janey," she said as she dumped a pile of mail and phone messages on my conference table. "You get Employee of the Month again."

"Morning," I said. "I know. I am totally pathetic, aren't I? Please don't answer that." I started going through the phone messages, placing the "fires—must be put out" in one stack, the "smoldering—keep an eye on" situations in another stack, and finally the "call if you feel a need to punish your-self" slips in another stack.

"By the way, the lights aren't on yet in Godzilla's office." MaryLouise cracked her gum loudly.

"You know Vivienne gets her hair touched up at Frédéric Fekkai on Tuesday mornings."

"You mean that neon yellow with pink undertones isn't natural?" MaryLouise snorted. "You need coffee?"

Before I could answer, I heard two unmistakable voices outside my office. My mother and Hugh. Instantly, my stomach started churning.

"You sweet Hughie, *you, you, you,*" Vivienne was saying in that little-girl voice that made me cringe. "Where were you when I was looking for husband number three?"

Probably in grade school, I thought.

Then Vivienne was standing in front of me, with Hugh, who had a bouquet of white roses that must have set him back two hundred dollars.

"Look who I brought. Quite possibly the handsomest man in New York," Vivienne said, leaning over to give me my morning kiss on the cheek.

She wasn't completely wrong about Hugh. Standing there with tousled blond hair, wearing faded jeans and a gray hoodie, Hugh looked exactly like a leading man should. He was definitely a dreamboat, a hunk, a catch. And, in theory at least, he was mine.

"I'm sorry. I'm *so, so sorry,* Jane," he said, managing to sound half-credible and sincere.

Even though I wanted to punch out his lights, I decided to play it a little cooler than that.

"What are you so sorry about?" I asked, eyebrows raised.

"Last night, of course. Are you kidding? I never made it to Babbo."

"No big deal," I said. "I had a very nice meal. Caught up on some work."

"I forgot I had a squash game."

"No problem. Squash is your life." Not even close. Mirrors were his life.

MaryLouise took the bouquet from him. "I'll go find a swimming pool to put these in."

After some meaningful, sixth-grade-style throat-clearing and pointed eye-rolling, my mother finally left too. Hugh locked the door behind her, and I frowned. What was this? Then he took me by both shoulders and kissed me on the lips. I sort of let him, and that royally pissed me off about myself. I bet even Door-mats Anonymous would turn me down. Oh, but Hugh was a good kisser, with those beautiful brown eyes up close and personal, Hermès Something Sexy misted on his neck and collarbone.

"I really am sorry, Jane." His hand moved up and down my back, and his smile *was* adorable. "You do know I love you, don't you?" His voice was warm, his eyes ultrasincere. Maybe he was possibly telling the truth.

Leaning forward, he feathered kisses against my neck. Suddenly I felt safe and warm all over, the way I used to feel with Michael. *Why on earth was I thinking about Michael?*

I dragged my mind back to Hugh, Hugh, who was nuzzling my neck. Ridiculously handsome, charming, insanely romantic-when-he wanted-to-be Hugh.

Then I remembered something.

Hugh was an actor.

Nineteen

MICHAEL HAD NEVER DONE anything like this—not even close—but that morning he'd trailed Jane at a safe, non-nutjob distance as she walked from her apartment to an office building on West 57th Street. He wasn't sure what he was doing; he knew only that he felt compelled to do it. On 57th Street, he immediately recognized the building as the place where Vivienne had housed her production company, and apparently still did. *Oh, Jane, don't go in there! Not into the lair of the Wicked Witch of the West Side! She'll trap you with her dark arts!*

But in Jane went.

And then, against his better judgment, so did Michael. *What are you doing?* he thought, and he nearly said it out loud. *This is the time to walk away.* Right now, right here. This is where you stop the madness.

But he didn't. He couldn't. And as he scanned the lobby directory, it became clear that Vivienne was more successful than ever. ViMar Productions now took up two entire floors. *She must be wickeder than ever.*

He watched the grown-up Jane as she made her way through the lobby. She waved to at least half a dozen people, and they waved and smiled back, or chitchatted briefly. It hit him that she hadn't really changed: She was still getting let down by people, and yet she was friendly and warm. Clearly she was well liked by everyone who knew her. Everyone except the schmuck who'd stood her up last night.

Then Jane disappeared into an elevator, and he watched the floors rush from LOBBY to 24 in a matter of seconds.

That's when Michael made the fateful decision to wait for Jane. Why? He didn't know. Would he even try to talk to her? No, of course not. Well, maybe. Just maybe. In the meantime, he had passed a Dunkin' Donuts about a block away, and he was thinking about a couple of Bavarian Kremes.

After the doughnut break, he went back and hung around Jane's office building, feeling stupid for lurking but unable to tear himself away. At about 12:15 the elevator doors opened, and out she stepped. She wasn't alone. Unfortunately, a very good-looking guy had his arm around her waist. Jane removed the arm, and Michael guessed that this was the loser himself: McGrath.

They went out the front door, and he was right behind them. Even if Jane happened to glance back, she wouldn't recognize Michael. She'd forgotten him. That was how it worked. Trying to look nonchalant, Michael stayed close enough to catch bits of their conversation. She and McGrath were talking about something called *Thank Heaven,* which Michael assumed was one of Vivienne's productions.

"Jane, *Thank Heaven* is the key to everything I've worked for, and I don't think you're treating it seriously," Michael heard McGrath say, or, rather, whine.

"That's not true, Hugh," said Jane. "I am taking this seriously. You know how passionate I am about *Thank Heaven.*"

Hugh. This guy's name was Hugh. What was she thinking? Never trust a Hugh. Jane was with a man who had the most ridiculous name on the planet, a name that was always, always misunderstood. *How are you, Hugh? Baby, it's Hugh. Hugh never know. It had to be Hugh.*

Shaking his head, Michael stayed with them as they turned into the Four Seasons restaurant. Inside, Michael went to the bar, ordered a Coke, and watched them be seated, knowing beyond a doubt that trailing Jane wasn't a good idea to start with and was getting worse by the minute.

Michael watched their table across the restaurant with growing irritation as Hugh did all the talking, Jane all the listening. When he wasn't lecturing her, the creep was working the room. *Hugh* shaking hands with a magazine publisher. *Hugh* hugging a talk-show host. *Hugh* pontificating over the wine list. What did she see in this jerk?

Then, as Hugh and Jane were about to begin lunch, a pretty young waif of a woman approached their table. She apologized for interrupting but held out a piece of paper and pen for Hugh to autograph. That meant he was some kind of celebrity. Like, an actor-slash-model? A weatherman? Maybe he'd been in *Saw II* or something?

He stood up, flirtatious, charming, nauseating. Michael watched and couldn't believe it. Jane's face and neck had gone red. She was clearly uncomfortable, but Hugh didn't seem to notice.

Finally Michael just couldn't stand it anymore. He paid for his soda, then left Jane with her Hugh. He didn't know what Jane was doing, but she was a big girl. If that was the kind of stupid, superficial relationship she wanted, then maybe she and Hugh deserved each other.

Twenty

WHILE HUGH FLIRTED with an obnoxiously pretty and pathologically thin fashion model who had seen *his* play four times, I pretended to study the dessert menu, which, sadly, I knew by heart. *God save me,* right then I would have killed for a piece of Chocolate Dome Cake.

But I shouldn't. I wouldn't. I really, really couldn't.

Take your mind off it. Okay, I had to get back to the salt mines for a *Thank Heaven* preproduction meeting. I needed to introduce our possible financier, Karl Friedkin, to some of the creative people — casting agent, costume designer, set designer. No Dome Cake for you, I told myself sternly. Ix-nay on the ome-day ake-cay.

Hugh air-kissed his skinny, doting fan, while I paid the fat check for our lunch.

"Mind if I don't go back with you, Jane?" he asked.

"I need to hit the gym." Unconsciously he preened in the mirror over the bar, stroking his perfectly smooth cheek and checking out his different angles. Of course, I have the kind of face that doesn't even have angles, from any direction.

"No, that's fine, Hugh," I said. "I'm good."

Actually, I was telling the truth. The less he knew about the behind-the-scenes development of the movie, the better. Since he'd played the role on Broadway, Hugh definitely thought that he should play the lead in the movie. So did my mother. The two of them had been lobbying hard for me to contract him for the part. I pretty much disagreed with every fiber of my being. Hugh was all wrong for movie close-ups; he just wasn't that kind of an actor. He just wasn't Michael.

Hugh gave me a kiss on the cheek, remembering only at the last second to make it real and not an air kiss. "Later, babe," he said, and then he was gone, glowing smile, glowing tan, slicker than a snake on a rainy day.

Firmly dismissing the longing to get a piece of ake-cay to go, I hurried back to 57th Street, arriving right on time, of course. How very Jane of me. After making sure everyone knew everyone else, I started the meeting. Once I began talking, my nerves settled, and I felt pretty much in charge of the project.

"We're all very excited by the way the film is shaping up," I said, encouraged by everyone's rapt attention. "An A-list director is just about on board. I believe we'll have the formal studio go-ahead by the end of the week."

Everyone spontaneously burst into applause, and it warmed my heart. I knew this project couldn't mean as much to my creative team as it did to me—how could it?—but I relished their enthusiasm and support.

Then the conference-room door flew open.

"No need for applause," Vivienne said in sugar-sweet tones. "I'll just sit here quietly and listen. Go ahead, Jane-Sweetie. Proceed."

My heart sank, but I straightened my shoulders, determined to carry on despite knowing that the likelihood of my mother sitting and being quiet—or for that matter, listening—was about the same as some weird comet suddenly striking Earth and melting the fat from everyone's thighs. It would be nice, but it wasn't going to happen.

"I'd like to talk about the sets," I said. "Clarence? What are your thoughts?"

"I think we're going to have to build an exact replica of the Astor Court," Clarence said.

"I was hoping that we might actually shoot at the St. Regis," I said. "Both to save money and for added authenticity. Couldn't we? Somehow?"

"If I could jump in for a second, Jane-Sweetie," my mother said, "I think we should build the set. It'll give us more control over the camera angles and lighting."

Of course she was right, and suddenly there were sage nods around the room. Nobody ever disagreed with my mother.

The costume designer spoke next. "I was thinking that the little girl should always wear white when she's with her imaginary friend at the St. Regis."

White would perfectly capture the idea of childhood innocence, I thought. "Yes, that sounds good," I said. "And it's the sort of thing the actual little girl *did* wear."

Vivienne interrupted again. "Janey, you have to remember, this isn't a biographical film. I think variety in the wardrobe would be better and would add color and texture to the screen. I'm certain of it, actually. Trust me on this. I have no ego. I only speak the truth."

And here's a "well, duh" realization: It was suddenly clear to me that my mother and I had entirely different approaches to making this film. Also, my mother was determined to exert her influence over what was supposed to be "my" project. What a shocker that was.

"I have a question," said Karl Friedkin.

I turned to him in relief. "Yes?"

"So who will be playing the make-believe man?" Friedkin asked.

"Well, he wasn't exactly make-believe," I said. "More imaginary."

A moment of silence ensued. Oh, great, I thought, trying to come up with a quick way to backtrack and finding nothing. The silence stretched on. Very uncomfortable. I began to blush. Now they probably thought I was crazy. Excellent: a perfect end to a perfectly heinous day.

My mother rose, smiled thinly, and walked to the door.

The casting agent said, "I floated the role past Ryan Gosling's agent, and she was very positive. Of course there are so many other excellent choices: Matt Damon, Russell Crowe, Hughs Jackman and Grant. Even Patrick Dempsey."

My mother turned in the doorway, knowing every eye was on her. Looking right at me, she said, "You play the Hollywood name game as much as you want, kiddies, but I have a feeling that the perfect leading man is right under your noses."

Everyone looked confused. Except me.

I'd just had lunch with the Hugh who Vivienne had already chosen for *Thank Heaven,* and it wasn't Jackman or Grant.

Twenty-one

YEARS AGO when he and Jane had wanted to escape from her constrictive and smothering Park Avenue world, they would take the crosstown bus to the Upper West Side. What a terrifically funky and eclectic world it had been back then, before the baby boomers with their Maclaren strollers. Wide-eyed, Michael and Jane had explored secondhand clothing stores and West African restaurants, Spanish bodegas and Jewish delis, all mixed together and coexisting in harmony.

Now, Michael couldn't help thinking, that same neighborhood had all the character and charm of a suburban mall in central Ohio. Goldblum's Dry Cleaners had become a Prada. Johannsen's Hardware was a Baby Gap. The "World's Best Bagels" place had turned into a fancy soap store. As Michael thought of those hot, terrific bagels now, all he could taste was soap.

Only one really terrific place remained from the old Jane and Michael days: the Olympia Diner, at the corner of Broadway and 77th. It was run by third-generation Greeks who still managed to serve up the greasiest eggs, the fattiest bacon, and coffee so strong you had to brush your teeth after you had a cup. Michael thought it was quite possibly the best food in all of New York, way better than Daniel or Per Se.

It was worth a visit just for the sign in the window: YES! YES! YES! PANCAKES ALL AROUND YOUR CLOCK!

Since Michael had been back in New York this time, the Olympia had become a Saturday-morning ritual. Today he was there with Owen Pulaski, as payback for the party at which he had met Claire de Lune. He'd had a really nice time with her—talking about Jane, apparently.

"So, what happened, Mike?" Owen asked as they walked to a booth on the Broadway side of the diner. "I saw you letting the lovely Claire talk your ear off. Then, *poof,* the two of you were gone off into the night." He grinned and punched Michael's arm.

"We talked," Michael said. "That's all. Just talked till about four or so. She's terrific. Only twenty-two and wise beyond her years."

"Talked, eh?" Owen gave Michael a knowing glance. "I bet. I bet you were up all night, talking about women's shoes. Or maybe the Yankees, right? Not the Jints. You dog."

Owen leaned across the table, and there was that irresistible smile of his, probably the same one he'd had since he was a boy. "Tell you the truth, Mike. I've never been with a woman who wasn't a sex object for me. And, buddy, I was *married* once. For. Two. Years. Which should qualify as a first and second marriage."

"Really?" Michael asked in astonishment. "All women are sex objects to you? Seriously?"

That smile of Owen's was back, the twinkle in his eye. "Now, don't be judging me, Michael. Don't be judging me."

"No, I'm not, Owen. It's just... I don't know... there's so much more to women than that. Sure, the physical, but also that connection between two people. I think that love can be great."

"Ah, you *think*," said Owen, seizing on that. "But you don't *know*, do you? So there's a little bullshit tossed in there? Just a *little?*" He pinched his big fingers together, giving Michael the devilish Owen smile. The twinkle, the dimple. Michael almost felt seduced.

Owen laughed. "It's great, isn't it? The *look!* My

secret weapon. Years of practice, son. Years of practice."

Michael turned his attention to the morning crossword while they waited, and Owen took the sports section, occasionally snorting and muttering out loud about teams, athletes, and horses who had personally let him down.

"Give me a five-letter word for 'feel deep love,'" Michael said a couple of minutes later.

Owen didn't look up. "Horny."

"And we're surprised you're single?" said Patty — shapely, very cute, long blond hair — who often waited on Michael at the Olympia and whom he was crazy about.

Owen laughed, not at all put off. "What's good today, honey? Besides you?"

Patty raised one eyebrow and took out her pad.

Michael said, "What makes you think he's single?"

"Get the eggs Benedict," she told Owen. "Real Holland rusks." Turning to Michael, she said, "He's got that look."

"What look?" Michael asked. This was the kind of stuff he loved, the get-to-the-heart-of-humanity info.

"That *single* look," she said, tucking her pen behind one perfect, shell-like ear. She looked Owen up and down as if he weren't conscious. "Kind of hungry."

Owen gave her his killer grin. "Hungry for you."

Patty rolled her eyes, and they ordered. She nodded and swept off, blond and graceful, as Owen watched her every motion.

"Patty's very sweet. Single mom, has a little girl who's four," said Michael pointedly as soon as she was gone.

Owen smiled. "Only one kid? I always wanted to find a single mom with at least three or four." He winked at Michael. "Just kidding, podjo. Don't be judging me, Michael. I like Patty. She just might be the one."

Suddenly Michael was sorry that he'd brought Owen, his grin, and his twinkling eyes to the Olympia.

"Don't go and hurt her," said Michael. Not quite a serious warning, but almost.

"Don't be judging, Mikey," said Owen.

Twenty-two

I STARED AT MYSELF in the bathroom mirror, feeling like a soldier marching off to war. The pressure was on, but I had done it to myself this time. I had less than forty-five minutes to do a complete *Elle* makeover, and I needed the works—hair, clothes, makeup, accessories. If they had a pill that made you lose fifteen pounds in forty-five minutes but shaved five years off your life, I would have taken two.

I was meeting Hugh at the Metropolitan Museum, and I needed to look my absolute best, which in my case equaled, well, presentable. There was a cocktail party and reception there for a Jacqueline Kennedy fashion retrospective. I would be on Hugh's arm, which meant that I would be watched closely, even jealously in some circles.

Okay, first, set the mood: I put John Legend's *Once Again* in the CD player and cranked it. If that didn't inspire me, I was SOL. Ah, yes! That was much better.

Second, face the enemy. In my bathroom was a cabinet that held nothing but unopened makeup. Here were the bottles and tubes, lotions and potions, that Vivienne regularly gave me. After thirty-plus years, she was still somehow hoping that I'd turn from ugly duckling into gorgeous swan. *Not going to happen, Viv. Not today, not any day.*

Third, arm yourself. I took a deep breath and opened a package of Clinique Dramatically Different moisturizing lotion. I smoothed it into my skin in clockwise circles, as directed. So far, I was not seeing a dramatic difference. But I persevered. Next came a thin base of Barely There foundation, which was guaranteed to give me a perfect, porcelain finish. Hmm. With the blotches hidden, my skin looked, oh, let's say twenty percent better. Not exactly great but an improvement, at least to my psyche.

Finally I did the best I could with Bobbi Brown mascara, eyeliner, and lipstick. Was Bobbi Brown a man or a woman? No clue.

Fortunately, and amazingly, I had good hair color, a kind of bubbly blond, and, because of my mother's relentless urging, I could rest assured that I had a very good haircut. "Without a good haircut, everything else is for nothing," said Vivienne. Then, of course, she had added, "And you need all the help you can get."

Throwing caution to the wind, I took a few big scoops of Calvin Klein styling mousse and ran my fingers through my hair. The curls fluffed up and framed my face. I don't know whether it looked good or bad, but it looked different...and modern...and not like Plain Jane.

Suddenly my mind flashed back to when Michael and I were inseparable.

"War paint," Michael had said that when he'd seen Vivienne dressed to the teeth for a Tonys ceremony. I'd giggled, but Vivienne *had* been dazzling, a slender blond goddess whom I could never hope to resemble.

Now, looking at myself in the mirror, I saw with surprise that in fact I did have hints of Vivienne in my face. I had her cheekbones, or at least I would if I lost twenty pounds. My eyes were larger, rounder, and blue, but I had her long, thick eyelashes. My nose was more pronounced, but it was definitely more like hers and not my father's.

I'd never noticed any of this before. I remembered Michael looking down at me with love, saying, "You're a beauty," and sounding as though he really meant it. Is this what he had meant? Had he seen my mother in my face?

Or maybe he'd thought I was beautiful for myself. Nah.

Jane! Keep on task! Throwing my shoulders back, I flung open the doors to my walk-in closet, trying not to feel as if there were an eager crowd in there hoping to see me devoured by lions.

Oh God, it was worse than I thought. My panicked eyes took in the sea of beige and black and earth tones. I had nothing remotely sexy or even colorful.

Wait a minute. Wait one minute! What had we here?

Pawing through some out-of-season coats, I spied a couple of retro Chanel cocktail dresses, pushed way to the back. Vivienne (of course) had given them to me back when I was a teenager. I yanked one out and examined it. It looked like something straight out of a 1950s society magazine, hot pink, with a tight, fitted bodice and a full, flared, flirty skirt that stopped right at the knee.

"Some night you'll be totally bored with everything you own, darling, and you'll want to wear one of these," she had said. "Mark my words."

She'd been right, of course. She'd picked out the perfect thing. She was totally saving my butt (the same butt that hadn't seen a StairMaster since God knew when).

I put on the dress, loving the silky fabric. Then I couldn't zip it up.

On a mission now, I dumped out my lingerie drawer onto my bed. Under my sensible bras and full-coverage briefs was a one-piece foundation garment, which, with any luck at all, was made of Kevlar and would do the trick.

I struggled into it.

I put on the dress.

No go with the zipper.

I got a pair of pliers from the kitchen junk drawer. The zipper was no match for them, and the bonus was that the too-tight bodice gave my boobs nowhere to go but up, up, up. As long as I didn't need to bend down or take deep breaths tonight, I was golden.

The only thing more daring than my decision to wear the pink dress was my decision not to wear a jacket with it. If my arms were a little fleshy, let them be. In the best of worlds and the best of lights, maybe I would look voluptuous.

I couldn't even bring myself to peek in the full-length mirror in the hall. What if I looked like a fat kid in a Halloween costume? There was no time to change anyway.

I took the elevator to the lobby, and I was off to a good start. The doorman said, "You look lovely tonight, Miss Margaux. Would you like a cab?"

"No thanks. I think I'll walk."

I kind of want to be seen for a change.

Twenty-three

I WALKED WEST on 75th Street, then made my way uptown, and for once in my life I felt as though I actually belonged on Fifth Avenue. As I climbed the steps of the Metropolitan Museum, I definitely felt different. My heels clicked rapidly on the stone stairs. I felt exotic, glamorous, womanly. I didn't feel like Jane.

I spotted Hugh standing at the top, leaning against a column as if posing for a Ralph Lauren ad. His jacket was slung over his shoulder and he was slouching just so, pretending not to notice the many admiring glances sent his way. He stood up straight as soon as he saw me, and his eyes widened.

"My God," he said, "what have you done with Jane?"

I laughed, pleased that he had noticed, and he

kissed me on the cheek. Then lightly on the lips. Then he stood back and examined me again.

"What *did* you do to yourself?"

"I decided I was tired of you always being the pretty one," I said flirtatiously, trying on a new behavior as well as a new look.

"You mean, the *only* pretty one," Hugh countered, squashing my happiness a bit. He laughed, to soften it, but he just hadn't been able to resist, had he? No wonder he and Vivienne got along so well.

He took my hand in his, though, and led me toward the grand museum doors. We made a good couple, and I actually fit in with all the well-dressed men and glam women parading into the reception.

I was happy, I looked good, but one disturbing question kept turning over in my mind: Did I really want to go to all this trouble for the rest of my life?

Twenty-four

THAT JACKIE KENNEDY sure knew how to pick out clothes.

Each outfit was more incredible than the last. And with every sip of my apple martini, those dresses of hers grew even more incredible. The sky blue Givenchy. The solid gold Cassini. The beige Chanel daytime suit that would never go out of style.

The best thing that happened to me that night—except for Hugh being amazed at how good I looked—was being greeted by a stone-faced Anna Wintour, editor of *Vogue,* who said, "You look well, Jane." High praise indeed.

"My knee is killing me from tennis this morning. Let's sit down," Hugh finally said.

So we sat at a tiny cocktail table in the museum's Great Hall. I wanted to stand, to be seen for once in my life, but on second thought my Jimmy Choos could use a little break.

"I'm going to smoke a cigarette until someone comes and throws water on me," Hugh said.

Before he had time to light it, I looked up and saw Felicia Weinstein, Hugh's smarmy, pushy agent, walking toward us. She was arm in arm with Ronnie Morgan, Hugh's equally sharklike business manager. My eyes widened.

"Jane, look," said Hugh, all surprised delight. "Felicia and Ronnie! What a coincidence. Hey, why don't you guys join us? That's okay, isn't it, darling?"

I was speechless, but Hugh was already scooting over to make room for his entourage.

With cold humiliation, I realized that I had been set up.

I had practically snapped a wrist getting into my body-slimmer for Hugh's agent and his manager. I couldn't believe it. I should have known something was suspicious—Hugh had been on time for once.

"What are they *doing* here?" I whispered, already feeling a sharp pain in the pit of my stomach. Suddenly my apple martini felt like lead marbles.

"Felicia mentioned they might pop by," said Hugh.

My eyes narrowed. Felicia was too much—too much hair, too much makeup, actually cracking gum.

"What," I muttered, disgusted, "d'she leave her pimp outside?"

Hugh gave me a sharp glance but didn't respond.

As for Ronnie, he had on a *Miami Vice* T-shirt-and-jacket combo, perfect for "taking a meeting" at Chateau Marmont in Hollywood—in the mid-1980s.

"Fancy meeting you two here," Ronnie said as he delivered a moist kiss to my cheek.

"Fashion lovers all," Felicia said, hardly bothering to look at me.

"I'll get drinks," Hugh said cheerfully, and the Cowardly Lion popped up as if he were spring-loaded. "These apple martinis are delicioso."

"No," Ronnie said. "I work for *you*. I'll get them."

But Hugh insisted, walking away, and I was left sitting with those two big sharks at a very small table.

"You look so *in-ter-es-ting* tonight," Felicia said. "Pink, huh."

"Is that a compliment?" I asked.

"You decide, darling."

I decided "no." My skin was crawling, and I thought I might break out with hives.

Ronnie chuckled awkwardly and removed his jacket, which made him the only man in a room of five hundred people in his shirtsleeves.

"Jane, now that we're together, let's *chat,* shall we?"

he said with false heartiness. "Felicia and I were going to get on your calendar this week, but since we've happened to run into you..."

Hugh returned. "Apple martinis all around," he said, and beamed.

"Hugh, this was so lucky, us running into you like this," Felicia said.

"Yes indeedy," said Ronnie. Had they *practiced* this routine, the three of them?

"No point beating around the proverbial bush, Jane," Ronnie went on, turning to me. "Felicia and I...and Hugh, of course...well, we just need to know when you'll be signing him officially for the lead in the movie of *Thank Heaven*. We have other offers, but we want this one. Hugh does, anyway. And you know what else? Hugh deserves it. Don't you agree? You must. We all do. And so does Vivienne."

I was furious...and nervous...and sad. But mostly furious.

"I don't think this is the time or the place to discuss it," I said, feeling my face turn to stone.

"I think this is an excellent place and time," Hugh said, his eyes steely, any trace of a smile vanishing.

"Oh, let's talk it out, Jane. It's a fun subject at a fun event," Felicia said.

It was *not* a fun subject, and it was no longer a fun event.

"You *do* plan on giving me the part in that movie, don't you, Jane?" Hugh asked, his eyes boring into my face. "How could you not?"

"We need to examine all our options," I said stiffly. *Because you weren't right in the play, and I don't want you to screw up my movie.*

My whole romantic future was going up in flames, right now, under the watchful, ferretlike eyes of Felicia and Ronnie. I hated this so much. Suddenly it felt as if all five hundred people in the room had stopped talking at once.

"I'm just not sure if you're right for the part, Hugh." I finally spoke in the quietest voice. "I'm being honest."

I reached for his hand, but he pulled it away.

"You need to change your mind," he said intently, his jaw set. He'd never quite bullied me before, and I wanted to whack him in the head with my Judith Leiber clutch.

"I was right for the stage," he went on. "I should have won a Tony."

I wanted to say that he was, at best, only okay in the stage version. He hadn't even been *nominated* for a Tony. It was the little girl who had won the hearts of the audience, and the critics. Hugh's reviews were, well...respectable. His best moment had occurred when he was dressing to meet the little girl at school. For about five minutes he'd had to walk around with his shirt off. He was very good at that.

Suddenly Hugh stood up.

"I want that role, Jane. I deserve it. I made that play work. *Me.* I'm leaving now. If I don't, I'll pick up this fucking table and throw it against the wall. You're just playing some stupid game! Fuck you, and fuck Jacqueline Kennedy!"

Suddenly I was alone with Ronnie and Felicia. *What had happened to this night?*

Ronnie spoke: "I'll go get us another drink."

"Not for me," I said. "I already feel like I'm going to throw up."

A minute later, I was listening to my heels clicking through the Great Hall, then down the steep museum steps.

I felt like a stupid, chunky idiot, in a much-too-young stupid pink dress that was now being stained by my tears and mascara.

Twenty-five

MICHAEL WAS BECOMING comfortable with
his stalker status. Maybe a little too comfortable.
This is the last time, he promised himself. *It all ends
tonight.* An hour or so earlier, Michael had been
floored when Jane walked out of her apartment,
looking like a million bucks. He'd shadowed her as
she walked from her apartment to the Metropolitan
Museum.

There was a determined movement in her walk,
he noticed. A strut in her step. And that hot pink
dress...She looked as though she'd recovered from
Hugh. So maybe she was okay now. Maybe Michael
could just be happy for her as he trailed along at
a safe distance. If Jane was okay now, then it was
time for him to disappear again.

* * *

SKIP FORWARD ABOUT AN HOUR, and he was following her back *down* Fifth Avenue. Jane was walking alone again, but much slower now, her shoulders hunched, no spring whatsoever in her step. When she cut over to Madison Avenue, she stopped and stared aimlessly in several store windows, including one of those places that sell cigarettes and Tic Tacs.

Somehow she seemed very alone to him, and so sad, so miserable. Obviously something bad had happened at the Met. No doubt it had had something to do with that creep Hugh McGrath.

More and more, Michael thought that he was to blame. He'd made her a bunch of lofty promises and predictions when she was just a kid. And they simply hadn't come true. He had told her, and he'd believed, that someone special would come along for her. Well, obviously that hadn't happened. Could he help her now? No, he didn't think so. Jane wasn't his responsibility anymore. He couldn't interfere.

But he definitely wanted to. His heart went out to her. He wanted to hold her and comfort her, just the way he had done when she was little. At 76th Street, Jane crossed Madison Avenue, then walked through the side entrance of the Carlyle Hotel, and into Bemelmans Bar.

Now what should he do? What were his options?

Michael waited a few seconds, then decided to follow her inside.

That pink dress of hers was easy to track. And there Jane was at the bar.

Michael sat at the far end of the bar, positioned beyond two fairly large, out-of-towner types. From what he could tell, they were drinking the house Scotch with Budweiser chasers and gulping handfuls of peanuts.

Jane ordered a gin and tonic. She looked beautiful sitting there, in a tragic, Russian heroine kind of way.

C'mon, Jane, chin up! You're so much better than this.

For a crazy second, he considered going over and talking to her. She wouldn't remember him, after all. He would be just some guy. In truth, he didn't know what to do. Which was very unusual. In fact, he'd never been unsure before, about anything.

What was he doing sitting in Bemelmans with Jane Margaux? Well, not exactly with her, but wishing that he were.

It made no sense. It was maddening, confusing, and just not a good idea. No, actually this was insane!

"What can I get you, sir?" the bartender asked.

"Uh, nothing, I'm afraid. I just remembered...I was supposed to meet somebody somewhere else. I'm sorry."

The bartender shrugged, and Michael stood, feeling awful, unlike himself. Head down, he started for the door. He turned and took one last look at Jane.

What a beautiful woman she'd become. Just as special as ever.

"Good-bye, Jane," he said, and then he left without talking to her. It was the only way. In fact, he wished he'd never seen her again.

Twenty-six

THE GIN AND TONIC was cold and fizzy and crisp. Tanqueray cut by lime. Just right. Was there any better place than Bemelmans to sit and think and feel disgustingly sorry for yourself?

I was a thirty-two-year-old woman who had everything and nothing going for her at the exact same time. I had a good job that was theoretically fascinating, but it consumed my hours and days and gave me almost no personal satisfaction.

I had a wealthy, successful mother, but she treated me like an idiot child and called it love. And worse, I desperately loved *her* anyway.

I had a boyfriend. Yes, that was for certain. *Had* a boyfriend. Past tense.

My mind began racing in a lot of bad directions all at the same time.

Maybe my goals were too long-term. Maybe

I should figure out a way to be happy, not for a lifetime, but for an hour or two. Maybe there was somebody out there who wanted to sit around with me, and order in Japanese, and not hate watching a DVD of *You've Got Mail* or *The Shawshank Redemption* for the fourth or fifth time.

Suddenly I felt a tap on my shoulder, which almost made me jump and scream. In that suave, woman-of-the-world way I have.

I turned to see a couple of men grinning somewhat moronically. Their loud, checked sport jackets looked out of place in the Carlyle Hotel, but then they'd probably look out of place anywhere. I didn't need this kind of attention right now.

"Evening, ma'am," said Thing One. "My friend and I were wondering if you wanted some company."

"No, thank you," I said firmly. "I'm just winding down after a long day. I'm good. Thanks."

"You seem all alone," said Thing Two. "And kinda down in the mouth. Seems to us, anyway."

"I'm really fine, more than fine. Thank you for asking." I even faked a smile for them. "Fine and dandy, that's me."

"Bartender, the lady could use another drink."

I looked the bartender in the eyes and shook my head. "I really don't want another drink. And I don't want to be talking to these guys right now."

"Maybe you two gentlemen want to move back down to the other end," the bartender said, leaning on the bar.

They shrugged, but as they walked away, one of them said, "This bar sure has some uppity hookers."

The bartender and I looked at each other in shock, and then we both laughed. It was either that or cry. In my pink designer dress, five-hundred-dollar shoes, carefully applied makeup, and chic haircut, I looked like a call girl? How much money did call girls make these days? Still, I turned around on the barstool to examine myself in the wall mirror. The image was mostly a blur of people and also reflected the colorful Bemelmans murals over the bar.

Smiling faintly, I looked at my reflection, with my ruined eye makeup, my pink nose. I would be one lame call girl.

Then I noticed something else. I squinted, feeling my heart instantly kick into high speed. It was completely, totally, utterly impossible. For a moment, my eye caught the image of a man leaving the bar. He seemed to be looking at me.

Of course I was wrong— but I would have sworn it was Michael.

As fast as I saw him, I lost him out the door.

Now *that* was really crazy.

I took a sip of my drink. My hands were shaking

when I set it down. That man—it was ridiculous. My subconscious had used a trick of the light, a shadow, to create an image of the person I missed the most, wanted most to see.

Okay, I was truly worried. Was I going off the deep end? I was starting to *see* things. How unhappy did a person need to be before her subconscious would kick in, try to make things better? How bad off was I that I thought I had seen Michael?

Michael, who was imaginary.

Michael, who didn't exist.

Had I wished so hard for Michael that he had reappeared for a second?

Wake up, Jane. It had to be a trick of flashing light. Maybe a cigarette lighter.

I took a twenty-dollar bill from my purse and left it on the bar. Then I walked outside and headed home.

I *knew* I hadn't seen Michael, of course, but the much more important question was *why hadn't I ever been able to forget him?*

Twenty-seven

WELL, ON TO BETTER, and definitely more meaningful, subjects. On Sunday mornings, I worked at a women's shelter on East 119th Street, Spanish Harlem. No big deal, no Purple Hearts necessary, but it was something I could do to help out a little, and it brought much-needed perspective to my life. Six hours at the shelter, and I came home feeling blessed beyond belief. I kind of thought of it as going to church, only better—more useful, anyway.

So there I was ladling out scrambled eggs and beans, hard rolls and squares of margarine. Paper plates for the food, plastic cups for the orange juice. It felt good to know that these people would have full stomachs this morning. "Can you give my son more eggs?" a mother with a five- or six-year-old boy asked. "You do that for me?"

"Of course," I said. I gave him another scoop of eggs with a hard roll on top.

"Say thank you to the lady, Kwame."

"Thank you."

"You going to be able to eat all that, Kwame?" I gently kidded the boy.

He nodded shyly, and his mother spoke in a whisper: "Tell the truth, he eat some now." She took a wrinkled piece of tinfoil from a shopping bag. "Finish the rest for supper."

The line kept moving, hungry people coming, and I kept dishing out eggs for them, saying "Thank you, please come again," trying to make everybody feel as welcome as possible.

An old, good-hearted Italian woman from St. Rose's Parish worked alongside me, pouring orange juice and milk. "Look over there," she whispered, pointing with her elbow to the middle of the line. "She's just a girl herself." I spotted a rail-thin woman, no more than eighteen, if that, with a baby in a worn Snugli. A little boy clung to the woman's skinny legs. What really set her apart, though, were two black eyes and a soiled bandage twisted around her limp right arm. Stuff like that made my jaw clench and my stomach turn, to think that anyone would get away with hurting someone like that.

When she came to my spot on the line, I told her,

"Go sit down. I'll bring the food over to you and the kids."

"No, I can manage it."

"I know you can. Let me help anyway. That's my job."

I found a plastic tray and piled it with eggs and rolls. I took two cups and a full can of orange juice. I even grabbed three bananas from the kitchen, where the nuns kept fresh fruit for special occasions or delicate situations.

"Hey, thank you," the girl said softly when I got to her table and unloaded the food. "You're a nice white lady."

Well, I try.

Twenty-eight

FINALLY, THE LAST of the scrambled eggs went onto the paper plate of an elderly woman who had no teeth and wore plastic bags over her hands and her shoes. "Make it through another day," she kept repeating over and over. It was a little disturbing how deeply I related to that sentiment.

Just before noon, I stepped out into the crisp spring morning of a Spanish Harlem Sunday in New York. My arms hurt and my head ached, but there was something basic and good about feeding people who are hungry. It was beautiful everywhere I looked, everything seemed full of life and promise, which, considering last night's debacle, seemed like a miracle.

On the steps of the church were five little girls dressed like miniature brides, kids about to make their First Communion. Nearby, serious-faced men drank *cervezas* and played dominoes on wooden cartons. I inhaled deeply. The smell of fried churros was in the air, and corn on the cob, and chili.

I crossed over to Park Avenue, where the commuter trains come out of the underground tunnel, and where this ragtag Harlem neighborhood eventually turns into the fancy Upper East Side. I kept walking, feeling pretty good now. I was pretty much over last night at the Met.

As I crossed the next street, my own building came into sight, and some jerk began honking his car horn at me.

I turned around and saw that the obnoxious jerk was Hugh.

There he sat, looking bashful and apologetic in a shiny blue Mercedes convertible, his angel's face sending all rational thought fleeing.

Oh, how our eyes can tell lies to our brains.

Twenty-nine

THE ONLY THING PRETTIER than the navy blue, sun-dappled sports car was the man driving it, and he knew it. Hugh was wearing Italian sunglasses and a light brown leather jacket that looked so soft you immediately wanted to touch it. And to give him a "regular guy" look, a New York Giants cap with the visor bent at the sides, just so.

"Join me for a spin, beautiful." Delivered in a humorous tone I knew he'd stolen from Mr. Big in *Sex and the City.*

Hugh and the car made a lovely couple, but I was thinking I could do without either of them. After all, I didn't care. I really didn't. Well, I almost didn't care. Oh, damn it, maybe I cared a little bit.

"I'm supposed to meet my mother for lunch in an hour," I said coolly. "She's been a little under the weather lately." The words floated out without my bidding, but they sounded great.

"I'll get you back in an hour. You know I wouldn't dare piss off Vivienne."

"Hugh, after last night...I just can't—"

"C'mon. Come for a ride. I want to talk to you, Jane. I came all the way up here from the Village."

"I really don't know that we have anything to talk about, Hugh," I said, keeping my voice mild.

"I'm a changed man," Hugh said, channeling deep sincerity, "and I can even tell you why. Give me a chance to talk."

I sighed and looked reluctant for a full thirty seconds before giving in and climbing into the car. Hugh happily gunned it down Park Avenue.

Suddenly he swerved the SL55 to the left, and soon we were speeding along FDR Drive, which was moving just fine, but moving *where?*

"I've got to tell you what I always seem to be telling you, Jane."

If he said, "Give me the part," I swear, I was going to shove a pen right into his ear.

"I've got to tell you that I'm sorry," he said, totally taking me aback. "I'm so sorry, Jane. I didn't know what Felicia and Ronnie had planned, I swear to God. Then my stupid tongue and temper got the best of me."

My brain told me that couldn't be true, even as my heart was registering how incredibly sincere he sounded. I was starting to soften up a little bit, and I didn't like it. Trying to stay strong, I didn't respond, just kept my eyes focused on the horizon. We were going bumpity-bump over the Brooklyn Bridge now. Heading where? And why? On the other side of the bridge, Hugh drove to a spot with an incredible picture-postcard view of Manhattan. Honestly, the city looked as if it had been carved out of a perfect piece of silver. I'd never been here with Hugh, and I suddenly wondered who had been?

"I guess I assumed we were on the same wavelength about the movie part, Janey," he went on. "I saw myself in the role. I did it on Broadway. It's part of me. I assumed you just saw me as perfect for it too." He shot me a gorgeous smile, contrite and cocky at the same time.

Okay, as motivation it almost made sense. "You just weren't listening, Hugh." As usual.

He draped his arm over my seat and lightly stroked the back of my neck.

"You know, Jane, I also thought that this project, this little movie, could turn us into the team I know we can be. I pictured us working together. It would be fantastic. Together in our personal lives and in our professional lives. You know, I'd be there for you. I could help you, support you. I've thought about it a lot. It's my dream. Honestly."

His voice was low and sincere. He was holding my hand, rubbing my knuckles gently. What was going on here? I was getting a little dizzy. I was weakening, wasn't I?

He opened the glove compartment and reached in. My eyes almost popped as he pulled out a robin's-egg blue jewelry box.

Inside my chest, my heart seized. He couldn't . . . he wouldn't . . .

This, I hadn't been expecting.

When Hugh opened the Tiffany's box, there was a lovely diamond. It wasn't huge, but it wasn't small, either. I tried not to suck in a wheezing breath.

"Jane, I know we can be great again. I've got the ring, and you've got the movie. Let's make a trade, sweetheart. Do we have a deal?"

Time stopped. The earth tilted beneath me. Oh. My. Freaking. God. Oh, my God. No, this *didn't* just happen. I felt as if I had just been punched very hard in the chest. A long pause followed while my stunned brain tried to decide on a response: Instant tears? Rage? Pathetic humiliation? This had been my first and only marriage proposal, and I couldn't imagine it sucking more. Was Hugh insane, or was I just a much bigger loser than even I had suspected?

Hugh stopped smiling, watching my face.

Finally, my synapses started firing jerkily, and I searched for breath. "I'm sorry, Hugh," I said tightly, in a colossal understatement. "About so many things... giving you another chance, caring for you in the first place. And I'm most, most sorry about what you just said to me. *Let's make a trade, sweetheart? Do we have a deal?* How could you *possibly* say such a thing?" My voice had risen with each sentence, and I was aware of a strident, anger-constrained tone that should have made him run for the hills.

"I'm not a speechwriter, I'm an actor," he muttered. "Okay, maybe I didn't pretty it up enough, and I apologize. But I was going for direct honesty. Isn't that what you always say you want?"

"*Pretty it up enough?!*" I sputtered. "Are you *nuts?* Try 'biggest insult of my life!' Try 'worst disaster of a heinous proposal *ever!*'"

Hugh's face had gone cold and stony. "Jane, you're making a huge mistake in judgment. Maybe you should check with Vivienne."

I'd thought I couldn't be more stunned, but I was sadly mistaken. I was now officially more stunned. "Oh, Hugh" was all I could manage, starting to choke up. "Get me out of here. Take me home. Right now."

Hugh looked at me for several long moments, disbelief marring his handsome face. As if he couldn't imagine what I was so upset about. Finally he shifted his body back toward the steering wheel. He turned the key in the ignition.

"Then I'll see you around." He leaned across me, flicked my door open, then popped my seat belt loose. He leaned against his seat and waited, disdain oozing out of every pore.

"Whaaaat?"

"Get out." His tone was icy, his knuckles white on the steering wheel. When I didn't immediately move, he turned and started yelling. "Get out of my fucking car!"

My face burning, I jumped out of the car. He was throwing me out? And he was doing it in Brooklyn.

Without waiting for me to close the door, Hugh peeled out backward and sped away, kicking up gravel that hit my legs.

He had done it. He'd taken me to the middle of Brooklyn and then kicked me out with no ride home.

Strangely, I didn't shed a tear.

Not for the first six and a half seconds, anyway.

Thirty

HE HAD NOTHING but time. It was a beautiful day, and he was trying to kick his Jane habit, so Michael was headed out for a walk, maybe a movie. On his way out, he met Owen on his way in, coming up the stairs of the brownstone—with Patty, the waitress from the Olympia. *Oh, no. What have I done? Owen and Patty?*

They were a cute enough couple, except that Michael didn't trust Owen as far as he could throw him, and he really liked Patty. He didn't want to see her hurt by a confirmed womanizer.

"Hi, Michael." Patty beamed, as she always did at the restaurant. "I was hoping I would see you. I wanted to thank you for bringing Owen to the Olympia that morning."

"Oh, it was nothing. Best pancakes around, right? How are you guys?" He tried to send Owen a warning glance, like, Hurt this girl and I'll kill you, but Owen didn't meet his eyes.

Patty continued to smile and did seem happy. "I'm great. But this one, he's a diamond in the rough. He's funny. Another Dane Cook."

"I am not," Owen said, looking offended. "How could you think that? And *who's* Dane Cook?"

"See?" said Patty affectionately. "He *knows* Dane Cook's a comedian."

"Yeah, Owen's a card, all right," Michael said, wanting to come right out and warn Patty. Owen wasn't deliberately cruel, but Michael didn't see how this could end well. "Okay, see you guys."

"Bye!" Patty said, and Michael sighed and continued downstairs. He was nervous for Patty—and her little girl. Owen had flat out told him that every woman he'd ever known had been a sex object to him, even his wife. Great, that was great. Well, maybe Patty would save him from himself.

He looked back up the stairs at the two of them, and there it was, Owen's get-away-with-anything smile. Great. "Don't be judging, Mikey!" Owen called out, and grinned.

And God, *he* had brought them together. Some friend he'd been to Patty.

Once Michael was out on the street, he didn't know what he wanted to do. He'd decided not to go near Jane again, so that was out. It was the weekend, so the streets weren't as crowded, which was always nice. But the sight of Patty going up to Owen's had gotten to him, ruined his day before it had begun. Plus, in general he hadn't really recovered from seeing Jane in the first place.

Then he had an idea, he hoped not inspired by Owen. Maybe it was just the ticket to save the day.

He gave Claire de Lune a call, and she was home on this beautiful Sunday, and yes, she'd love to see him.

Thirty-one

I MUST HAVE EVENTUALLY found a cab in Brooklyn. It must have gone back over the Brooklyn Bridge. And it must have dropped me off at my apartment on 75th Street.

It must have happened, but I don't remember any of it very well.

I do remember seeing Hugh peel away; I remember the sharp gravel hitting my shins; I specifically remember giving him the finger. Next thing, Martin was holding open the door of my building, and I was staggering toward the elevator.

As I opened the apartment door, the phone was ringing, and I answered it in a daze, not even thinking that it might be Hugh.

"This is Jane," I said mechanically, kicking off my shoes.

"Jane-Sweetie!" My mother's imperious voice.

"Where are you? You said you were coming for lunch! I have that wonderful gravlax from Zabar's. Karl Friedkin is here. And I have photos from the new Valentino collection. And—"

"Sorry, I won't be there, Mother. I'm not feeling too great." Slight understatement.

"I think what you're feeling…is maybe Hugh McGrath?" my mother said playfully. "Bring the dear boy along. It will be fun. We can chat about *Thank Heaven*."

Oh, that was so not going to happen.

"Hugh isn't here, and I'm not feeling well. I'll talk to you later, Mother."

I didn't wait to hear her say good-bye. I immediately decided that I couldn't bear being in my empty apartment. Anywhere but here. Well, anywhere but here and *Brooklyn*. I changed my gravel-ruined pants for some jeans and a Music in the Park T-shirt and started walking downtown. No destination in mind.

In twenty minutes or so I was heading west. There was Hermès. And the Robinson Galleries. And then, my childhood home away from home: Tiffany's.

The sign in the window read: OPEN SUNDAYS, 11–6. Which I knew, of course. How many Sunday afternoons had Vivienne and I spent here, trying on estate jewelry and looking at diamonds through a loupe? I had probably been the only seven-year-old who could knowledgeably discuss facet proportions and the merit of an Asscher cut versus a brilliant one.

I leaped through the revolving door on 57th Street, timing it as if I were jumping rope. In no time I was near the Fifth Avenue entrance, and, all of a sudden, I was shopping for a diamond ring.

Thirty-two

WHENEVER I WAS INSIDE Tiffany's, memories rushed back. The feel of the carpet beneath my feet, the shine of the wooden panels, the heat of the lamps under the glass counters. This was the one place where Vivienne and I had gone alone, without her entourage, and we were like a real mother and daughter. This was where my mother seemed most herself—even more than when she was at the theater—and happiest.

I studied the display case as if I were planning a June wedding, which, oops, I guess I had put the kibosh on earlier today. The diamond rings were like a constellation, all lined up in a divine, predestined order: from the smallest, barely visible single-stone band to exquisite natural pink and yellow square-cut and pear-cut diamonds set in platinum, each ring worth more than some luxury automobiles.

"May I show you something?" a young saleswoman had appeared out of the ether. She was my idea of elegance in a simple black suit with a lovely string of pearls, everything just so.

"Um," I said.

I saw her surreptitious glance at the naked fingers of my left hand.

"You know," she said confidingly, expertly unlocking the case, "lots of women are gifting themselves with diamonds for their right hand." *Gifting themselves.* Now there was a phrase. It sounded so much better than, say, *ridiculously indulging.*

Yes, I had actually seen the ads in *Vanity Fair* and *Harper's Bazaar.* Every ring has its own meaning. A special day. A dream come true. A wonderful secret. Blah. Blah. Blah. But obviously the sales copy had worked on me, at least a little.

"May I see that one?" I asked, pointing to an elegant Tiffany Celebration ring, more than a dozen flawless diamonds set in a platinum band.

"It's beautiful, isn't it?" the saleswoman said as she delicately placed it on a piece of black velvet. The diamonds burned with an inner fire, and even when I was seven I could have told you that their cuts were perfection.

God, the ring *was* beautiful. So beautiful that it almost hurt my eyes. It hurt my heart, too.

"Try it on," urged the devil's handmaiden.

I slipped it onto the third finger of my right hand. Whew! I felt like a real grown-up. It practically made my wrist clunk down on the counter. It was truly, truly stunning. A Celebration ring indeed.

"It fits you perfectly. It won't even have to be sized," she said in a conspiratorial whisper.

I had been to Tiffany's enough to believe that the man in the gray suit standing next to me, the man pretending to be looking at diamond rings also, was a security guard. Did I look suspicious? Dangerous? I could only wish.

"What's the price on this?" I asked, feeling my heart lurch.

She whispered, "Thirteen thousand." Somehow she made that number sound like an unbelievable steal.

I calmly said, "I'd like to buy it."

As if she heard that statement every ten minutes, the saleswoman said, "Of course."

I handed her my credit card and IDs. The transaction went quickly, and yes, Virginia, there's a reason for that.

After reading my driver's license, the saleswoman asked, "Are you by any chance related to Vivienne Margaux?"

"She's my mother."

The saleswoman let out a knowing "I see" and

within a few minutes I was standing out on Fifth Avenue, the diamond facets on my hand catching the sun just perfectly.

I sneaked a look at my hand as I began walking downtown. I waited for the traffic light to change. I sneaked another look at my hand.

Then I glanced to my left.

There it was.

Just as inviting as Tiffany's.

Thirty-three

"THE ST. REGIS! I love the St. Regis," Claire said as she and Michael turned the corner of 55th Street and the hotel was revealed. He had picked her up at the place she shared with another model near Bryant Park. Then they had walked north on Sixth, then Fifth. He'd kidded that maybe he could buy her a little something at Tiffany's: another weird Jane memory popping into his head.

"Are you rich, Michael?" Claire asked, laughing.

"In spirit only," he said. Actually, all he had to do was snap his fingers, and he had most of what he wanted. Literally. Snap! And some cash would appear in his pocket. He didn't know how it happened, but why fight it? Anyway, Michael's needs were few; the simple life suited him best.

"Can we go in?" asked Claire.

"Absolutely. *We* love the St. Regis!"

And suddenly there it was, right in front of him: the Astor Court. Everything about the hotel restaurant seemed to have changed; and yet everything seemed exactly the same. Women in designer outfits, dads treating their kids to lunch, whole families attacking petits fours and Napoleons, tarts and crème brûlées.

"Will that be two?" the maître d' asked.

"Please. Two," said Michael, feeling his pulse racing just a little. Now, why would that be? It wasn't as though he'd see Jane here. Not even eight-year-old Jane.

He and Claire were seated at an intimate table for four, and within moments someone swept away the two extra settings.

"This is fabulous!" said Claire. "Somehow I've never been here, after five years in New York."

Michael smiled at her, glad he could give her this pleasure. His eyes examined every aspect of the room. It almost did seem to have been frozen in time. The music playing was "Love in Bloom," the trolley was piled high with desserts, porcelain trays were full of tea sandwiches.

Except that there was no imaginary friend eating melon, no eight-year-old girl devouring coffee ice cream with fudge sauce. It was as if the stage had been set, but one of the most important characters hadn't shown up.

Jane was missing from the scene.

What was he doing? Trying to recapture some of the happiest afternoons of his life. With Claire de Lune as a stand-in for a sad, brave, amazing girl who had kept his heart when he'd left her behind. He looked at Claire. "Is this okay?" he asked.

She beamed. "Of course! I love it, Michael! Any girl would. And in case you haven't noticed, I'm a girl."

He swallowed. "Yeah, well, I did notice that."

Thirty-four

THE HEADY RUSH of spending a fortune on a ring that could be used as a spotlight from a space station was starting to fade, leaving me a little jittery. Like any self-respecting addictive substance. Now I desperately needed to relax, to calm down. And yes, since this was go-to-hell day, to eat dessert. The St. Regis was the perfect place for all of the above. I was hanging on by a thread: My *ex*-boyfriend was an egomaniac and a complete and utter jerk; my *current* mother was making me crazy, and had been for decades; I had just spent a huge sum of money on a ring I didn't need. Beyond that, everything was just fine and dandy.

"Would you like to see a menu, miss?" the waiter asked.

How did he know I was a "miss"? Was it in my eyes? The way I held myself?

I needed to seize control. "No. I'll just have iced tea," I said virtuously. "Thank you."

"Of course."

Then my sanity returned. Virtuous, schmirtuous — too late. I was wearing a diamond ring that I had *bought for myself.* "Wait! Hold up. You know what? I'll have the hot fudge sundae. With coffee ice cream."

"A much better choice."

I was enjoying shooting diamond laser beams all over the Astor Court when the waiter returned with my ice cream sundae. The silver dish was bigger than Hugh's head. There was no way I could finish this whole thing—and ever hold *my* head up again in public, anyway. How had I managed to do it when I was eight years old? Maybe I had been a little pudgier than I remembered. Or no—much better—it had no doubt been served in a much smaller dish back then. Yes. That was the ticket.

The first luscious spoonful brought everything rushing back. It was all very Proustian, *Remembrances of Guilty Pleasures Past* and all that good stuff.

How I had loved those Sunday afternoons, here, with Michael, and at Tiffany's, wherever Vivienne wanted to go, as long as I was included.

My mother and her friends would sit gossiping or doing business, and Michael and I would wander into our own little imaginary world. Was that the last time I had actually felt happy? If it was, then I was more pitiful than I wanted to admit.

I took another spoonful, this time making sure that the ice cream was accompanied by just the right amount of fudge sauce. This was so, so what I needed. This, and the honking big ring on my right hand. I wiggled my fingers, letting it catch the light.

Speaking of pitiful, since I didn't seem able to avoid it, I had to admit that I still believed in my imaginary friend from childhood. What should that tell me about myself?

And then...

I blinked, looked away, and blinked again.

What the...?

I had noticed a couple sitting just a few tables away. A nice-looking couple. In fact, a perfect choice for the Jane-and-Michael game.

But that wasn't what was so shocking.

I put down my spoon, slowly wiped my mouth with a napkin, and really stared.

Suddenly my hands and knees were shaking, and my lower lip was quivering.

The man...? It couldn't be...

Michael?

I blinked my eyes rapidly again, like a cat in a cartoon. I started to perspire and continued to tremble.

"Michael" was with a very pretty woman with silky, minky dark hair. She was gorgeous, actually. One of those model-beautiful women who seemed like exquisite freaks of nature. Michael had always told me that he could be an imaginary friend only to children. Eight years old was the limit. That's why he had left me on my ninth birthday. What, had he gotten promoted or something? Could grown-ups have imaginary friends? If so, where was mine?

Or maybe...maybe it wasn't Michael after all. I mean, of course it wasn't Michael, who had been, after all, imaginary.

But it had to be. That smile was unmistakable. The amazing green eyes. He was as good-looking as ever, maybe even more so.

It crossed my mind that I was crazy.

Well, okay, maybe I would just run with that. What could I do about it now anyway? Call 911 on myself? It occurred to me: If I really was insane, then I wasn't responsible for my actions. It kind of freed me up in a way.

I stood up from my table and headed toward them.

If this man wasn't Michael...well, I'd throw my

arms around him anyway. I'd probably kiss him. I might even ask him to marry me.

The day he left me, Michael had said I'd never even remember him. He'd been completely wrong about that. I remembered every single thing about him. *And this was definitely Michael...*

Unless I had gone completely insane.

Could go either way.

Thirty-five

"IF I EAT this entire ice cream sundae, (a) it will be all your fault, not mine, and (b) I will not be able to get into the clothes for my shoot tomorrow morning. And (c) I'll be fired."

Michael laughed. "Ah, the silver lining. Then you'll go back to school full-time, graduate, and become a brilliant teacher even sooner."

She took a bite of the ice cream, a big bite, and made a funny face with food in her teeth, the kind that only gorgeous models and small children can make without grossing people out. Actually, maybe only models. "Is that what you think I should do?"

"Of co——" Suddenly Michael was staring across the room.

"Earth to Michael?" Claire said. "Ground Control to Major Tom?"

Michael was still staring, and thinking, *This can't be happening. Cannot. Must not.*

For a moment Michael panicked, then remembered that this was just a coincidence. She couldn't remember him. They never did. They always, *always* forgot. That was what made it bearable.

He busied himself with his menu, eyes down.

Then he felt her standing at his table. Feigning nonchalance, he looked up.

Her blue eyes were huge, her lovely face pale. "Michael," she said.

He didn't answer her. He couldn't put any appropriate words together yet. Or thoughts.

Jane spoke again. Not the little girl Jane, the full-grown woman Jane.

"Michael? It *is* you, isn't it? Ohmigod, *Michael? You're here.*"

Thirty-six

MY VOICE HAD COME OUT shaky and raspy, so that I almost didn't recognize myself. I was on the edge of being very, very embarrassed. "You *are* Michael?" I asked again, thinking that if somehow I was wrong, I would have to turn and *run*.

He took a deep breath, and then he said, "You *know* me? Are you sure?"

Oh God, this might just be really happening. "Of course I know you. I'd know you anywhere..."

And then he said my name, just that. "Jane?"

The Astor Court is a large room, but it seemed to be closing in around me. The sound in the room was a little off too. Everything was suddenly unreal, to put it mildly. This couldn't be happening, but clearly it was.

The beautiful woman with Michael was wiping her mouth with a napkin, and then she stood up at the table. "Ah, the mysterious Jane," she said, but she said it kindly. "I have to go, Michael. Thanks for the ice cream, and the advice." She gave me a smile, and I blinked, because she really was way more dazzling than I. "Take my seat. Please. *Jane.*"

Michael rose now, and I was afraid he was about to leave too. This time, I wouldn't let him leave as I had when I was nine years old. This time, I would take him down in a flying tackle, right here in the Astor Court, if I had to. Right onto the Oriental.

But Michael pointed to the empty chair, "Please, sit. Jane. Jane Margaux."

I sat, and then he and I stared at each other. It was like meeting someone out of your dreams, or fantasies, or a beloved character from a favorite book. How could this be? Any of it? There wasn't a logical answer that I could think of. Good thing I had given up on logic when I was twelve and realized I was never going to marry Simon Le Bon. Michael still seemed to be somewhere between thirty and thirty-five. I saw the exact same recognizable pattern of freckles across his nose. His eyebrows, his ears, his hair, and finally, his eyes—they were all the same. Those beautiful green eyes, the kindest eyes I'd ever seen. I'd looked into those eyes a million times, and I was looking into them now. So incredibly green.

The next question couldn't have been any more

honest on my part, and it was something I desperately needed to know. "Michael, are you imaginary?"

He looked uncomfortable. "I guess that's a matter of opinion."

"What are you doing here? How can this be happening?"

He threw up his hands. "Honestly, I have no idea. I'm just in New York...waiting...for my next assignment."

"Oh, so that wasn't her?" I asked, leaning my head toward the exit.

"You of all people don't have to ask that," said Michael. "You know what I do, and it isn't with grown-ups." He frowned. "That didn't come out right."

"And you just ended up at the Astor Court? On a Sunday? And I wound up here too?"

He shrugged helplessly, looking as bemused as I felt. "Looks like it, huh."

In a way, it was comforting that he seemed as confused by this as I was.

"Jane."

I couldn't believe it was him, Michael, saying my name.

"How did you remember me? That isn't supposed to happen."

"I don't know," I said, feeling a weird sense of calm coming over me. "You said I'd forget you, that

I'd wake up and not remember you. But the next day I woke up and realized you were really gone, and it was like a safe had fallen onto my chest. I couldn't get out of bed. I cried for days."

Michael looked at me, appalled.

"I just...never forgot you. I've thought about you every day for twenty-three years. And now here you are, back again. It's...unbelievable." To put it mildly.

"I'm so sorry, Jane," Michael said. "They just... always forget. I never would have caused you such pain if I could have helped it."

I looked into his eyes, feeling an eight-year-old's sense of hope. "Well, I'll think of some way you can make it up to me."

Thirty-seven

THE NEXT THING I was fully aware of was that
Michael and I were walking up Fifth Avenue on
a sun-drenched Sunday afternoon and it was like
being awake in a dream. Oh, I don't know what it
was like, really. But it was incredible and exhilarat-
ing and confusing and disorienting.

When I was six or seven, I had known that
Michael was funny and clever and really nice to me.
But now, as a woman, as a grown-up, I realized
there was so much more to him than that. For one
thing, he was a terrific listener, which put him at the
head of the pack of everyone I had ever dated.

He said, "Tell me everything. Tell me everything
that's happened to you since your ninth birthday."

So I did, trying to make my life sound ever so
much more interesting and exciting than it had been
when I was actually living it. I found I loved making

him laugh, and he laughed quite a lot during our walk together that afternoon. Once we were out on the streets of New York he became very loose and relaxed. And so did I. More or less. Sort of.

With a grown-up's sense of awareness, I realized that Michael loved life and people. He could see the funny side of just about anything, and he was accepting of it, and not cruel. He could laugh at himself, and he counted himself among the ridiculous. I guess I would have to say that he laughed with people, not at them.

"So who was she?" I asked about the brunette back at the St. Regis.

"I don't even remember another woman. What other woman?" Michael said, smiling. "She's just a friend, Jane. Her name is Claire."

"And she's a *friend?*"

"Not that kind of friend...or the other kind either."

"And what's that red mark on your neck? Vampire bite?" I asked. "Do I want to hear this?" Not that I was jealous. Of my childhood imaginary friend. God, I guess I had really, really cracked. Well, I was going to run with it.

"I do a little boxing," he said.

"Huh," I said, trying to picture it. "Well, I myself spar with my mother on a daily basis, so that's another thing we have in common." He threw back his head, and I laughed, and the piercing pleasure I got from that was almost painful.

This was definitely Michael, Michael from my childhood, but now that I was grown up I could enjoy him in a whole new way. His intelligence, the wit, and his looks...my God! There was even something sexy about his boxing, the bruise on his neck, in a totally unmodern, un-PC kind of way. His smile had always been contagious, always filled me with happiness, and it still was, and did.

Of course, even as my heart pounded with a sense of discovery, I left room for the possibility that he would disappear at any moment, that Michael would suddenly turn to me and say, *"You'll forget all about me, Jane. That's the way it works."*

But it hadn't happened like that. Maybe it wouldn't again. I could hope.

"Oh, hey, there's the Met," Michael said. "It's open for another hour."

Was it less than twenty-four hours ago that I had spent one of the worst nights of my life in there? It felt like a year. But right now, I was eager to go back. Because with Michael, anything was possible.

Thirty-eight

"WHERE SHOULD WE GO FIRST?" I asked
him, when we stood in the massive entry hall of
the Met.

"I'd like to show you—" Michael began, then
laughed self-deprecatingly. "I mean, I'm sure you've
seen it, a million times. But I always wanted to see
it with you. Okay?"

"Yes." Frankly, at that moment he could have
said, "I think I'll eat a bunch of cat food. Join me?"
and I would have said yes. Michael took my arm.
It seemed a very natural thing for him to do, but it
made me shiver and feel almost light-headed—in a
good way. Except, of course, if I actually *did* faint
dead away. That would be not so good.

Arm in arm, we proceeded up the grand staircase.
I loved being with him here, but I was aware that it

didn't actually matter where we were, because I had to be dreaming, didn't I?

We turned left, walked through a large wooden doorway, and then we were standing in one of the most beautiful rooms in the world. Enormous canvases of Monet's water lilies covered the walls, surrounding us, taking us to a different world.

"Why do things this beautiful make me want to cry?" I asked Michael as I leaned into him. It was an unguarded question, one I'd never have asked of Hugh.

"I don't know," said Michael. "Maybe beauty, true beauty, is so overwhelming, it goes straight to our hearts. Maybe it makes us feel emotions that are locked away inside." He blinked and gave a bashful smile. "Sorry. I've been watching *Oprah* again."

I smiled back, delighted with this man who could actually laugh at himself. The exact opposite of Hugh: *not* Grant, *not* Jackman, *not* in my life anymore.

We walked around the spectacular room, filling our eyes and our hearts, not speaking for a few moments. After a while, it seemed that we both knew that it was time to leave.

"I'll walk you home," Michael said. "Do you mind?"

Did I mind? Of course I didn't mind. "No, that'd be great," I said. "It's not far from here, over on Park. In the Seventies."

"I know," he said.

"How do you know that?" I asked, surprised.

He paused. "I just know, Jane. You know how I am. I just know certain things."

As the afternoon turned into evening, the air got cooler, and the sky grew darker. We walked east, toward Park Avenue, but Michael didn't hold my arm anymore, and I began to dread saying good-bye. I didn't know if I could bear to. I knew I wouldn't have a choice.

On 80th Street we passed an exquisite building. Through its glass doors, we saw that the lobby was filled with French antiques, the walls covered in gold leaf. In the middle of the lobby was a large enameled pot holding the largest gardenia bush I'd ever seen.

"Oh," I said. "I love gardenias. Their scent. They're so pretty."

"Keep walking," Michael said. "I'll catch up."

Nervously praying he wouldn't disappear, I walked slowly, trying not to look back. A few moments later, Michael was back at my side, holding a single white gardenia. Its fragile edges were tinged with the faintest pink, and the scent perfumed the air all around us.

"How do you do that?" I asked.

"What? Get a flower for you?"

"No. Be so...perfect." I inhaled my gardenia's sweet scent, feeling suddenly close to tears.

Not responding, Michael took my arm again, and he felt familiar and warm.

We continued down Park Avenue, and I was trying to elongate every second, walking more and more slowly. But we couldn't put off the inevitable, and then we were in front of my apartment building. "Evening, Miss Margaux," said Martin, "Oh, and evening, sir." Martin gave Michael a look, almost as if he'd seen him before, but that was impossible.

I was dying to ask Michael up, but it seemed too brazen, too presumptuous, too *Vivienne*. The only thing more awkward than the sudden silence between us was the polite handshake we exchanged. But I couldn't let him just fade off into the night.

"Michael, I have to ask," I blurted. "I'm sorry, but I have to. Are you going to go away again?"

Michael paused, and I felt my head filling with extreme pressure, as if my ears might pop. Then Michael took my hand again and smiled kindly.

"I'll see you tomorrow, Jane. I...I miss you already," he said.

Thirty-nine

I HAD A FAINT SENSE that it was morning, and that I was waking up, and that something about my life had changed dramatically. Then I remembered Michael, and my eyes opened wide. Please, God, let it not have been just a dream, I begged silently.

Feeling fragile, like glass, I slowly turned my head toward my bedside table. There was my white gardenia, the one Michael had given me yesterday.

I touched the flower to make sure it was real—*it was*—and then I sat up and swung my legs over the side of the bed. It hadn't been a dream.

So this is how "happy" feels, I thought. The energy, the automatic smile. This is what it's like to look forward to the day, to believe there could be good things coming. It was a new and different feeling.

Out in the kitchen, I poured myself a large glass of orange juice. My answering machine was blinking urgently at me, and I drank my juice and hit the Play button before it had a heart attack.

"Jane, it's me. What can I say? I'm so, so sorry. I don't know what came over me. I feel just awful about the car thing in Brooklyn. Call me and—"

Erase.

"Jane-Sweetie, I think it was a tad cavalier of you to skip lunch. I didn't get to give you your kiss. And you know, Karl Friedkin is vitally important to—"

Erase.

"Jane-Sweetie, I was just thinking about that fourth-scene entrance in Thank Heaven. *I don't know what Hollywood hack you got to write this screenplay—"*

Erase.

I didn't bother with the other nine messages. I just pressed the Erase button.

I took a shower, letting it run colder than usual. The cold was invigorating, and I felt so alive, skin tingling, blood pumping. As I dried off, for once my eyes didn't avoid the full-length mirror. You know, I wasn't half-bad. My skin was fresh and rosy. My wet hair was thick and healthy. Was I overweight? Hell, no. I was voluptuous, with a woman's curves. This is what a woman looks like, I told myself.

I slipped on pale purple silk panties and walked to

the closet, already knowing that I wouldn't be wearing any of my usual black skirts and shirts today.

I slipped on my favorite pair of soft, comfy, faded jeans. I pulled on a white blouse that I'd always liked. I hooked an old cowboy belt around my waist.

Now I was carefree and happy, comfortable in my own skin, for maybe the first time since I was eight years old.

Just before I left the apartment I held the gardenia to my face and smelled it.

Then I slipped on my new diamond ring and headed for the office.

Forty

"HERE ARE YOUR MESSAGES. Here is your coffee. And that jackhammer-like noise is the sound of your mother's high heels coming down the hall."

My secretary, MaryLouise, handed me a mug with a *History Boys* movie logo on it. I had loved the play *and* the movie, so there was hope for *Thank Heaven,* right?

"Mmm. Thank you. This is delicious," I said, taking a big gulp of coffee.

"Good. I figure when they kick me out of here I can go work at a Starbucks."

"Maybe both of us," I muttered. "Baristas forever."

I began going through the stack of messages. Not surprisingly, the vast majority were from Hugh, and his slimy agent, and his sleazy business manager. The three of them had managed to generate eleven separate calls. They could kiss my denim-clad butt.

"I didn't even bother giving you the messages from—" The door flew open in the middle of Mary-Louise's sentence. Vivienne was standing there in full fury.

"*Your mother.* And may I present her now."

Vivienne stood with both hands on her size-two hips.

It took all my self-control not to say, "Are you ready for your close-up, Miss Desmond?"

First, she gave me my morning kiss.

Then, it started.

"It is almost noon, Jane. Where the hell have you been? And for God's sake, what are you wearing? Are you going to a *rodeo?*"

I continued riffling through the messages. There was nothing from Michael.

"I asked you a question," Vivienne said loudly, leaning on my desk, so as to better get in my face. "In a very civil tone, I should add."

"Have you got another Splenda?" I asked Mary-Louise.

She nodded and opened a desk drawer.

My mother looked speechless for just a moment, but of course that was too good to last. She got her second wind as I stirred the Splenda into my coffee. "Well, I certainly want to hear where you were yesterday *and* yesterday evening," she said firmly.

"I called you so many times, I think I broke the redial button. You don't have the common courtesy to return your mother's call? Is your machine broken? Or is this some kind of teenage rebellion, twenty years too late?"

At my continuing silence, Vivienne changed tacks. "I heard about what happened with poor Hugh and Felicia and Ronnie," she said, making it sound like "Hiroshima called. They said you bombed them." "I don't know what on earth is wrong with you. Do you know how angry they all are? And rightfully so. Because you happen to be stubborn, and you happen to be *wrong*. I know show business like you'll never know it, and Hugh McGrath is perfect for that movie role. Without Hugh, there *is* no movie."

"Why, thank you, Mother," I said, but she didn't get the *Hugh-you*-confusion thing. I took another gulp of coffee and let the phone messages drop like confetti into the wastepaper basket.

"You're lucky I'm here to do damage control," my mother went on. "We're going to have to meet with poor Hugh and his people at lunch. Call Gotham Bar and Grill. We'll meet them down there at one. If they'll let you into the place dressed like a cowgirl."

I drank the last of the coffee.

"Are you finished, Mother?"

Her eyes blazed.

"First, I'm a grown woman. I was *out* yesterday. With a friend. Where we were is absolutely none of your business.

"No, my machine is not broken. But I was busy. This is not teenage rebellion, since, as I mentioned, I'm a grown woman. This is me, acting like a grown woman. I suggest you join me.

"Now, onto Hugh, *not* Grant, *not* Jackman, and the role in the movie. That discussion is closed. We will never ever talk about it again. *Thank Heaven* is my property. I got the funding. I got the studio involved. And I want someone better than Hugh *McGrath*. Do you hear me, Mother? *I never want to discuss it again.*

"So I'm afraid lunch with Hugh and his minions is out. I won't respond to your critique of my outfit because I decide what I will wear, and I'm not really interested in anyone else's opinions." Except Michael's. "And you know what, Mother? I think I look great."

Vivienne gaped at me as if I had sprouted antennae. She sputtered and stammered for a few seconds, then turned around and stormed away, slamming my door first, then the door to her office down the hall.

"Will that be all?" MaryLouise asked.

"I think that about covers it."

Forty-one

WHAT WAS GOING ON WITH HIM? More to
the point, what was going on with him *and Jane?*

Hell if he knew.

Michael got into the shower and turned the water
to hot. He was going to see Jane today. He felt nervous and excited and happy and kind of filled with
dread, all at the same time. It was the most emotion
he'd ever experienced, and he felt kind of sick, actually. He stayed in the shower for a long time, then
wrapped himself in a towel, wiped the fog from
the mirror over the sink, and began to shave.

Feeling as if he didn't recognize the face in
the mirror, he covered it with shaving cream and
began swiping smooth tracks with one of those
superefficient five-bladed razors.

And then it happened.

Something that had never happened to him before. The unthinkable.

He cut himself shaving.

First time ever.

A dot of red puffed near his chin, then mixed with the shaving cream to form a patch of pink.

He watched this phenomenon as if he were watching a miracle, like water suddenly gushing from a rock, or the dinner with the loaves and the fishes. He finished shaving, rinsed his face, and stuck a tiny piece of toilet paper on the bloody spot.

Incredible. A toilet-paper bandage! Another first.

He dressed quickly in whatever was clean and walked out into the hallway. He turned to lock the door behind him, just in time to catch Patty from the Olympia, sneaking out of Owen's place.

"Hey, Michael," she said, blushing prettily in an old-fashioned way. "You nicked yourself shaving, huh?"

"Hey, Patty. Yeah, I cut myself. Isn't it something?"

"Um, I guess, sure. Well, gotta go. My mom's staying with Holly. My little girl. I have to take her to school. Then off to work at the pancake factory."

"Be careful out there," Michael said. He wanted to point to Owen's apartment and say, "Be careful in *there,*" but he didn't.

Patty grinned. *"Hill Street Blues.* I loved that show.

That's what the sergeant always said, right? Later, Michael."

He followed Patty down the stairs, but when he got to the street she was already gone. He hoped she'd be okay. He felt a little responsible, somehow. Maybe he shouldn't.

Finally he started to focus on his own day.

He had no idea where he was going this morning, but he knew it had something to do with Jane.

"I cut myself shaving!" he marveled out loud, and got some funny looks from passing strangers. "Guess you had to be there."

Forty-two

NORMALLY (IF YOU COULD SAY THAT), he had coffee and pastries with "friends" in the morning. But today he needed to see Jane again, to talk to her. At least one more time. So he took a long walk and ventured into the building where she worked, which had at first seemed like a good idea but now was starting to feel like a big mistake, one of a series. *What was he doing here? What did he hope to accomplish?*

"Hello," the woman at the reception desk of ViMar Productions said, startling him out of his fugue. "You must be an actor, right? Do you want to drop off your résumé?"

Michael shook his head. "Why would you say that?"

"Uh, have you ever looked in a mirror?"

He was trying to decide what to say next when

a scary image from the past came striding through the big red swinging doors behind the reception-ist. It was Vivienne, and God, the woman was liv-ing testimony to the fine art of plastic surgery. How many tens of thousands of dollars had been spent to pull that skin into such taut smoothness? Talk about miracles: She hadn't aged a day.

There was a touch of plastic-surgery shininess to the forehead; the cheekbones stood out a little too prominently. But she looked good. A little frailer, but still quite striking. And energetic, of course.

Vivienne focused on him. Michael knew that even though he had seen *her* a thousand times, she was seeing *him* for the very first time.

"Well, hello," Vivienne said, turning on the full-wattage charm. "I'm Vivienne Margaux. I know all the leading men in New York. So why don't I know you? Don't tell me you don't speak English."

"All right, I won't tell you," Michael said, and smiled pleasantly.

"A million-dollar smile, too," Vivienne said, ex-tending her hand. Michael took it. It was soft and smooth. Good Lord, she'd even had plastic surgery done on her hands.

"I don't know why our paths haven't crossed before. But it's a pleasure to meet you. Who are you here to see?" she asked, the smile never leaving her face, her head tilting to one side in a coy, schoolgirl manner.

"A friend of mine works here," Michael said.

"Oh. Really? Who's your friend? If I might be so bold."

"I'm here to see Jane," Michael said.

The smile disappeared. "I see," she said. Just then, with perfect dramatic timing, Jane walked into the reception area.

She froze for just a second, surprised to see Michael at the office. Then a lovely, slow smile came across her face, and Michael couldn't look away from her. She walked toward him and gently peeled the piece of tissue from his chin—as if it were the most natural thing in the world to do.

"He feels pain" was all she said.

"He does. And he bleeds."

Vivienne spoke up. "I just met your *friend,* Jane-Sweetie."

"Good," Jane said. "What's his name? He won't tell me."

"Michael," answered Michael.

"Michael what?" Vivienne asked.

"Just Michael," Jane said, and then she pushed the button to summon the elevator.

"Oh, like Sting or Madonna."

"That's right," said Jane serenely. Michael could

tell that Vivienne was burning for more information, but if Jane didn't want to indulge her, he certainly wouldn't.

"Ready for lunch?" Michael asked Jane.

"Starving."

"Jane, you just got here," said Vivienne. "We have meetings and phone calls—and this thing with Hugh is *not* settled."

"Okay, bye," Jane said sweetly, as if she hadn't heard her.

The elevator doors whooshed open, and she and Michael stepped in.

As the doors closed, Michael said, "We almost didn't make it out of there alive, Bonnie."

"Almost, Clyde. But we did. Don't look back. She'll turn us into pillars of face powder."

"I'll try not to," said Michael.

Forty-three

IF I COULD TAKE one experience in my life and make it last forever, I'd choose the moment that I saw Michael waiting for me in the reception area of my mother's office.

Not seeing him at the St. Regis for the first time.

Not walking up Fifth Avenue with him.

Nope. It would be the moment at the office. *Because that meant he was real.* And it made everything else real: Yesterday at the St. Regis. Our museum field trip. The gardenia that he gave to me. It had all actually happened. Which probably meant there *was* a Santa Claus, an Easter Bunny, a George Clooney.

"Let's get far away from here," I said to Michael.

"Okay. Where would you like to go?"

"Paris. Except I have to be back for a two o'clock meeting."

"Then Paris is probably out. Let's grab a cab, see where it takes us."

Michael snapped his fingers...and a cab stopped for us. *Interesting.*

"What was *that?*" I asked, my eyes wide.

"Honestly, Jane, I don't know. I've always been able to do it."

Ten minutes later we were walking around the West Village. First we stopped at a favorite of ours from the old days, Li-Lac Chocolates, at its new location on Eighth Avenue. I was so happy that it was still around. We bought chocolate truffles. Michael said it was "for after lunch." I told him that he couldn't tell me what to do anymore, and I ate one before we'd even left the candy store. So did he.

"Copycat," I said.

"The most sincere form of flattery."

We walked to Hudson Street and went into a store that sold nothing but amazing, antique cast-iron banks, like the kind in which you put a coin in a dog's mouth, then press a button, and the dog's tongue flips the coin into a juggler's hand.

"Jeez," Michael said. "This bank costs nine hundred and ninety-five dollars."

"Money's no object," I said grandly. "Would you like it?"

"Don't go showing off, rich girl," he said. But he looked pleased, and then right there in the middle of the store he pulled me into his arms and held me close, not speaking. At that instant, I knew exactly what I wanted out of life: *this. This* feeling, *this* happiness, *this* embrace.

We ate lunch in a delightful French restaurant that was called, simply, French Restaurant. Sitting there, eating chicken and *pommes frites,* drinking wine, we talked, and talked freely, easily, as if it were the most natural thing in the world. Us. Being there together as man and woman. Or woman and whatever Michael was. An angel?

We had lifetimes to catch up on. I told Michael about my four years at Dartmouth, where I was the only person in the entire school who refused to ski. He laughed when I confessed that the week I graduated, I joined a religious cult. Weight Watchers.

Michael said, "You don't need Weight Watchers, Jane. You look great. You've always looked great. Don't you know that?"

"Honestly," I said, "no. I've never known that."

I actually didn't tell Michael *everything*. Even though I told him all the best stories about what it was like to work for Vivienne, I didn't mention the success of the stage play *Thank Heaven*. Or that we were going to start shooting a movie about a little girl and her imaginary friend. Who just happened to be based on Michael and me.

When I finally got Michael to open up and talk about himself, he was charmingly modest, but also very discreet. He told me just a little about a few of his favorite assignments over the years. Twin boys in North Carolina, a woman senator's daughter in Oregon, a few appalling stories about a precocious child actor in L.A., someone I actually had heard of.

"I have a lot of questions about this 'friend' thing," I told him.

"Unfortunately, I don't have a lot of answers. I wish I did, Jane. You have no idea."

It wasn't a satisfying answer, but it was probably the only one I was going to get. Then I asked Michael something even more personal that I was dying to know. "Were you ever involved with anyone? Romantically?"

He shifted in his seat and shrugged. "I meet people," he said, not answering my question. "I like people, Jane. All kinds of people."

"And I'll bet they like you."

Michael didn't seem uncomfortable. He just seemed, well…reserved. And mysterious, of course.

"Let's go do something," Michael said, taking my hand. "Doesn't matter what." And he snapped his fingers for a cab.

Forty-four

IT DIDN'T MATTER what we did that day. We could have been digging ditches, and I would have been thrilled.

But we did something much better than digging ditches: We Rollerbladed over the hills of northern Central Park, where the blacktop was smooth and the traffic was sparse. We flew like angels on cement, barely avoiding runners, bicycle riders, dog walkers and their raucous packs of barking dogs. And all the while, I was delighting in his company and thinking, *What is happening here? Surely it's never happened before to anybody else. There has to be some logical explanation. Yet I might have to accept that there isn't.*

I hadn't been on Rollerblades since I was ten years old. I remembered that my mother called me a "clum," that is, a person with no natural grace. I did not seem to have improved much with age. At 96th Street, I was practically touching the ground as I tried to make it to the top of one of the steepest hills in the park. My calves and thighs ached. And then suddenly we were at the tip-top of the hill, flying downhill fast, fast, completely out of control. "Michael!" I screamed.

He grabbed my hand. "Trust me!" he yelled back.

So I did. And amazingly, we didn't crash, didn't wipe out. Michael was taking care of me again, as he always did.

Safe and sound at the bottom of the hill, we flung ourselves onto the thick grass, panting, a few feet away from an old woman in a wheelchair. She was there with a nurse-companion in a starched white uniform.

"I thought you had a two o'clock meeting," Michael said suddenly, looking at his watch.

"I did. I missed it." I felt a singular lack of concern. It was interesting.

The old woman was watching us, smiling now. Her companion fixed a shawl around her and began pushing the wheelchair away.

The woman turned and called, "Good luck to you two. You make a lovely couple."

I agreed. I looked at Michael, but his face gave nothing away. "Are we a couple?" I asked Michael, holding my breath at his answer.

He laughed lightly. "A couple of nutjobs maybe," he said.

Not what I wanted to hear, but I dropped it.

For dinner we had hot dogs in the park, hot, spicy, and doused with mustard and relish. We walked and talked and eventually we were at my apartment building again.

"Well, here we are," I said, with crackling wit.

We stood outside the entrance to my building, and Martin the doorman discreetly moved away from us. *Yes, I would ask Michael to come up to my apartment now. Of course I would. And Martin would approve.*

But as the fateful words were about to come tumbling out of my mouth, Michael leaned in close. Yes, I thought. Oh yes, please. His face was only an inch or so from mine, and my breath caught. I'd never seen him so close, his smooth skin, his green eyes.

Then he suddenly pulled away, almost as if he were afraid of something.

"Good night, Jane," he said. "It was a perfect day, but I think I'd better go now."

He turned and walked away quickly and didn't look back at me.

"I miss you already," I whispered.

To nobody.

Forty-five

GOOD NIGHT, JANE . . . I think I'd better go now.
How could he have said that? How could it possibly
be anything but a crazy, sleepless night for me after
a whole day of getting lost in Michael's eyes? I definitely didn't want to be alone in my apartment, but
here I was.

I walked to the living room and looked out at the
city as I munched a couple of Oreos. All right, *four*
Oreos. My floor was high enough to let me see over
the other nearby buildings, and I had a great view
of Central Park. New York had always been the right
place for me, but tonight it seemed even more so,
maybe because Michael was out there somewhere.
What was he, though? An "imaginary friend"? An
angel? A hallucination? None of those made any
sense to me. But I had no other answers.

Just then the phone rang. No way did I want to

listen to my mother or Hugh getting their panties in a twist. Let the machine pick it up.

First I listened to myself telling the caller to leave a message. Then I heard my friend Colleen's voice, the one who was getting married. We'd been in Book Club together, Movie Club, Rock Concert Club, Traveling Pet Club. Nowadays we probably didn't have so much in common.

"Oh, Janey, it's Colleen. I wish you were home. We still haven't talked since I told you about Ben."

I hurried to the phone and picked it up. "Colleen! I'm here. I was just coming in the door. How *are* you? I left you a message," I said. "I told you how I was dying to meet this big-shot Chicago lawyer of yours."

"I know, but I wanted to hear your voice," Colleen said, "in real time. I wanted to hear the real Jane."

"You got her, babe."

So we talked. When Colleen finished an hour or so later, I could have composed the *Chicago Tribune, New York Times,* and *Boston Globe* wedding write-ups on the two of them. Ben, the son of Dr. and Mrs. Steven Collins, had gone to BC as an undergraduate, then to Michigan Law. I wondered if Colleen would change her name, becoming Colleen Collins. Anyway, then Ben had worked for two years in the Chicago D.A.'s office. He had been introduced to Colleen by his sister-in-law at a party on Martha's Vineyard. He had an apartment overlooking Lake Michigan. Colleen, along with her cat, Sparkle, were moving in. When Colleen began telling me about the wedding-cake fillings, I broke in.

"Wow, it sounds like you've got everything all planned out," I said, trying to muster convincing enthusiasm. I loved Colleen, but if she told me she had two little fake mice in evening clothes on top of the cake, I'd probably throw the phone off my balcony.

"Oh, Jane. I did nothing but talk about me, me, me. You're so great to listen."

"No problem. That's what I'm here for. I love hearing you so happy." And if I was also a little jealous, that was my problem.

"Next time it'll be you calling me, with the same news. But, listen, what's new with you?"

"Not very much," I said. "You know, work, and trying to wrangle my mother into submission."

Colleen giggled. "As always."

Oh, I almost forgot, I think I'm falling in love with the most perfect man ever—sweet, funny, and incredibly good-looking—who just might be a figment of my imagination. Other than that, same old, same old.

Forty-six

MICHAEL WAS THERE the next morning.

Patiently waiting outside my building, just as he used to, so many years ago. In the flesh, so to speak. Not a hallucination. At least I didn't think so.

He had another beautiful white gardenia in his hand.

"Hello, Jane," he said, looking slightly rumpled and adorable. "Sleep well?"

"Oh yeah, out like a light," I lied. "You?"

We began walking side by side, in perfect rhythm, just as we used to walk to school each day. So was he watching over me again? Protecting me? Why? Did he even know why himself? Why didn't he have all the answers? He'd always known everything when I was little. He was never unsure, never hesitant. The fact that he seemed as confused about this as I was made him infinitely more human, somehow.

The weather was chilly for spring, and the sky threatened rain, but nothing could get me down today. I was *hopeful,* wasn't I? For the first time in a long, long while.

While we walked, we talked nonstop about everything and nothing, the past and the present—but not the future. Maybe talking with Michael was the best part of this, or of any, friendship or love affair. Although, God knows, I wanted to grab him and kiss him, and, honestly, do a lot more than that. He was a hunk in a way that an eight-year-old just couldn't appreciate.

"Jane! Want to go in there? For old time's sake?"

Michael was pointing across Madison Avenue to a familiar little shop of horrors called the Muffin Man. We had gone there on many a guilty morning twenty-some years ago and, to be perfectly honest, I had kept up the tradition.

"Once a sucker for muffins, always a sucker for muffins," I said. "Lead on."

As we waited on line in the shop, Michael said, "As I remember, the Apple-Cinnamon-Walnut was your muffin of choice."

"Still is." Among others. I'm not that picky, muffin-wise.

We each had a muffin, though I found that I wasn't really that hungry, which was odd but fine with me.

Michael had a coffee frappe, I had a decaf. What struck me most about me and Michael together was how little Hugh and I had ever talked about, or even had in common, really.

Once we were back on the street, and about a block from the office, the skies opened and it poured, coming down in buckets of icy rain.

"We can wait it out under that canopy, or we can make a run for it," Michael said.

"Run, obviously." Which was what I felt like doing, running and yelling out loud.

So we raced through the rain, through puddles up to our ankles, around people who were smart enough to have brought umbrellas. I wisely decided to keep the shouts of abandon to myself.

We practically fell through the doors of my building, drenched to the skin but laughing like a couple of kids, or at least challenged adults. Smiling goofily at each other, we naturally leaned closer, closer... *Oh God, I wanted this...to happen...so much.*

But.

"I'll see you later," Michael said, pulling back, losing his smile. He frowned. "Is that all right? Am I...bothering you?"

Oh yeah, you're bothering me, all right, I thought hungrily. But this time I wasn't going to let him dash off.

So I grabbed his arm, keeping him in place, then kissed him—on the cheek. The kiss was wet from the rain, but warm from my feelings.

"I'll see you later. I always want to see you," I said, and then I just had to add, "I miss you already."

That was me: taking chances, living large. Booorn to be wi-iild...

Michael gave me a last, affectionate look. Then I got into the crowded elevator and punched my button.

I couldn't help singing again, "Booorn to be wi-iild." I had no problem with letting my freak flag fly.

God, I was happy.

Forty-seven

MICHAEL WAS ACTUALLY really happy, in a tortured kind of way.

So he got together with a few of his best friends and told them about Jane, about how they'd met again, that she had bizarrely remembered everything about him. "The hot fudge sundaes, our walks to school, the terrible, terrible day I left her, *everything!*" The group was supportive but astonished. None of them had ever experienced anything like it. "Just be careful, Michael," said Blythe, whom he was probably closest to among them. "For your sake, and for Jane's. They're supposed to forget us. That's how it works. That's how it's always worked. Something strange is happening here."

"Oh, you think?" said Michael.

* * *

AT 5:45, he showed up at Jane's office, as he'd promised he would, and said good evening to his new friend, Elsie the receptionist.

"I don't think Jane's expecting me," he said.

"Think again," said Elsie. "She's expecting you. She's been expecting you for most of the day."

Elsie buzzed Jane, and a moment later she appeared, looking fresh and rosy-cheeked. Was she blushing?

"I told you I was bothering you," Michael said.

"He really is annoying," Jane confided to Elsie.

"Please. Annoy *me,*" said Elsie, who was well into her sixties.

The rain had started up again, but Michael had brought an umbrella. They headed all the way to a restaurant on the Upper East Side called Primavera, talking as if it had been months since they'd seen each other, instead of hours.

"So do you watch TV?" Jane asked, avoiding a puddle by walking closer to him.

"Mostly cable," Michael said. "Like *Deadwood* and *Big Love.*"

"I like those too!" Jane said. "What else do you do? What are some of your other interests?"

Michael thought. People didn't usually ask him about himself. As Claire de Lune had said, he was a terrific listener. "Um, I love live football games," he said. "I love Corinne Bailey Rae. NASCAR. Cézanne. The White Stripes."

Jane laughed. "So... everything."

He grinned. "Pretty much."

"What did you do today?" Jane asked, looping her arm through his.

"I met some of my friends," he admitted. "Friends who are... in the same line of work. And I went for a long run. And I napped."

"Well, isn't that special," Jane teased him.

"Hey, I'm on vacation, remember?" he said. By that time, they were at the restaurant, and it struck Michael: Was this a date? It felt like a date.

Forty-eight

"SO HOW WAS *YOUR* DAY?" Michael asked as soon as we had sat down and sent the waiter bustling off to get a bottle of Frascati for us.

I made a face. "Not too bad, considering that I had six separate meetings with Vivienne."

"Age sure hasn't slowed her down."

"Not much. Maybe a little bit. Lately, anyway. You know, I'm producing this film, a small movie, nothing major. A confection, I guess you could call it."

"Like *Chocolat*," Michael said, and he smiled. "I loved that movie."

There was a pause. I was trying to think of how to say this without giving too much away.

"Go on," Michael said. "Tell me about it. I like hearing about your work."

"You're probably the only one," I said, trying not to laugh too bitterly. "Anyway, we have a coinvestor on the film named Karl Friedkin. When I went past Vivienne's office this morning, after we got drenched in the rain, who should be sitting there but *Karl Friedkin?* So I asked MaryLouise, my secretary, about it. Know what she said?"

"That Vivienne is on the hunt for a new husband. Her fourth, right?"

I dropped the piece of Italian bread I'd been gesturing with and stared at Michael. "Amazing. Mary-Louise knew too. I'm the only one who didn't. I must be impossibly dense."

"No. You're just a nice human being. So your mind doesn't go that way without some provocation."

"And yours does?" I asked.

"Let's just say that I've seen your mother in action. You know that she loves you, though?"

I frowned. "Who wouldn't? I'm so *nice.*"

The waiter came by to take our order, which we split. I still didn't have much of an appetite, which was strange, but *good* strange. I didn't feel sick, just didn't feel like eating.

AFTER TWO ESPRESSOS and two Sambucas, we were heading south on Park. The rain had stopped, and I was using Michael's umbrella as a kind of walking stick. I started tapping it in rhythm, then suddenly I burst into a mortifying version of "Singin' in the Rain." It was like watching myself jump off a cliff but being unable to stop. "The suuun's in my heeeart, and I'm ready for looove…" Finally I got a grip.

"Sorry. Don't know what came over me. Just… goofy Jane," I said, hot-cheeked with embarrassment.

"I like goofy," said Michael. "Besides, you were being cute, not goofy."

See? Things like that made me love him more. Looking up, I saw that we were only a few blocks away from my building already. We continued walking, both of us quiet for a change. Would I ask him up? I wanted to. I really, really wanted to.

Trying to gather my nerve, I looked up at Michael, and then suddenly we had stopped and he was taking me into his arms again.

My eyes flew open, then fluttered shut as Michael slowly, slowly leaned down. I almost gasped when I felt his lips press against mine, and my heart gave a giant leap that I was sure he could feel. My mind, which I thought of as being in tatters now anyway, was completely blown. Oh, Michael…

In all my life, I'd never felt anything like it, nothing even close. Finally we broke apart. Staring up at him, pulling in air, I started to say—

But then we were kissing again, and I wasn't even

sure who had started it, only that Michael was holding my face in his hands. Then he held me tight, tight, in a little bear hug that I loved. We inched apart, but then kissed again and again. Finally we clung to each other, not speaking, and it occurred to me that I'd be happy to do this for quite a long time, like maybe the rest of my life. And also that I was feeling light-headed. I didn't want it to stop. Not ever.

Forty-nine

WHEN I GOT HOME from my "date" with
Michael, and I definitely thought it had been a
date, I didn't have a chance to process any of what
had just happened—because *someone was in my
apartment.*

The light in the foyer was on, and the kitchen
overheads, and at least one lamp in the living
room.

I had a crazy thought: that it might be Michael.
Who knows, maybe he could just make himself
appear somewhere.

Or it could be Hugh, because I thought he still
had a key to my place.

But if it *was* Michael, I didn't want to call out
"Hugh?" or vice versa. And what an ironic dilemma
for someone who was historically so bad with
relationships.

So I took a deep breath and said, "Hello?"

"Jane-Sweetie" came from inside the living room, and as I turned the corner, there was my mother, seated in one of my easy chairs.

"I thought I'd come over," she said, "for a little talk."

"Huh," I said, thinking I'd rather be smeared with honey and tied to an anthill. "How did you get in?"

"I still have a key from the remodeling."

Oh, and don't get me started on *that*. Suddenly the idea of a little post-date (and it had totally been a date) cocktail sounded like an excellent idea. I headed for the cupboard where I kept my embarrassingly inadequate supply of liquor.

"Can I get you something, Mom?" Vivienne winced at the name, but I loved to call her that, loved to know that I had an actual mom-type person. Plus, she'd just broken into my apartment, so "Mom" it was.

"Sherry," she said. "You know what I like, Jane-Sweetie."

So I went and got her sherry—and a stiff shot of whiskey for her put-upon daughter.

I sat across from her in the other easy chair. "Cheers."

"Jane-Sweetie," she responded, "I don't know what's going on with Hugh, or the other one, or any others there might be in your busy life." Her tone of voice suggested that the jury was still out on whether I had a busy life, or even a *life,* for that matter.

I just couldn't help interrupting. "Wow, I'm impressed! My busy life!"

"Please." Vivienne held up a hand, palm out. "Let me talk."

I nodded and took a sip of my drink, making a face as the liquid fire trailed down my throat. I missed Michael a lot. Already.

"Jane-Sweetie, what I came here to say is that—" My mother stopped, seeming uncharacteristically at a loss for words. I frowned and sat up straighter. Was she already engaged to Karl Friedkin?

"Yes?" I said encouragingly, dropping the attitude.

"Well, I'm not going to be around forever, and when I'm gone the company will be yours, and you can make whatever decisions you wish." She finished quickly, then took a deep drink of her sherry.

Okay, this was a completely new tack for her. I was starting to get concerned. "What do you mean, Mother?" I said.

"Don't interrupt. There's one more thing. I never told you this, but my mother died of heart failure when she was thirty-seven. You're thirty-two. Think about it."

Having said that, my mother rose to her feet, came

over, and gave me a kiss on the cheek, and then she left the way she'd come in.

What the hell had that been about? She thought I was going to die of heart failure? She'd been odd and unlike herself. Was she telling me that she had a heart problem? No, she would have been way more dramatic, complete with sweeping gestures and Bette Davis swoons.

As usual, Vivienne had gotten the last word.

Fifty

OKAY, OKAY, OKAY. I understood that pushing
the elevator button over and over again would *not*
make the elevator appear sooner. But I couldn't help
myself.

After my heart-pounding date with Michael (it
was *so* a date), and my weird talk with the mysterious Vivienne, I'd gotten about twenty minutes of
sleep. Now it was the next morning, and I was praying that Michael would be waiting in the lobby to
walk me to work. God, I wanted to see him again,
at least one more time. *Please. Please. Please. Let
him be downstairs. Don't let him be gone from my
life again.*

I considered running down the ten flights.

My Saks Fifth Avenue shopper—Vivienne's birthday gift to me (and what kind of gift says "you

embarrass me" better than a personal shopper?)—
had sent over a chic Lagerfeld suit, slacks and jacket
in a pale bluish green silk. I thought that I looked
okay in it, maybe even better than okay.

Damn it, I looked good! I'd even lost three pounds!

Three whole pounds. That had never happened
to me before.

The elevator finally arrived, and as I rode in it
I wanted to jump up and down to make it move
faster. *Jane. Please! Relax,* I told myself, and tried to
listen to my own advice.

When the elevator finally arrived at the lobby, I
put a smile on my face, but my heart was racing off
the charts. The doors opened. And then...

Only the morning doorman, Hector, was standing there.

"Good morning, Miss Jane," he said.

"Good morning, Hector. How are you?" *I'm devastated myself.*

No Michael in the lobby!

No Michael lurking outside the front door.

No Michael anywhere that I could see.

"May I get you a taxi?" asked Hector.

I stalled for time.

"I'm not sure. I may walk."

"Yes, of course. Beautiful day for it."

"Yes, it is lovely."

Maybe Michael was late. *Fat chance. Michael was never late. Not once when I was a kid.*

"I guess I will need a cab," I finally said. As I waited under the building's canopy, I looked up and down the street in the hope that Michael's face would suddenly appear in the sea of businesspeople and tourists and schoolchildren marching along Park Avenue.

But Michael wasn't anywhere in the crowd.

Had he gone out of my life again? If so, I would kill him if it took me till the end of my days. Or at least put a collar on him, with a little bell.

I mean, why had he bothered to come back in the first place?

Fifty-one

AS I WALKED into the reception area of ViMar Productions, I was feeling a little shaky, but strangely balanced, about myself, about who I was, and about where I ought to be going with my life. Was that the reason Michael had come back, because my confidence needed a little touch-up or, to be more honest, an overhaul? Was that what Vivienne was trying to say last night?

I saw Elsie waving from behind the reception desk.

"In your office," she said. "It's a surprise."

Oh yes, and I was so in the mood for something unexpected. I don't like surprises even on good days, and today it was about to make me run screaming down the hall. When I opened the door I was certainly startled, but *not* in a good way. It was Hugh. And he was seated at my desk, going through my mail.

"Now that you've done the snail mail, why don't you check my BlackBerry?" I said, and threw it on the desk.

He leaped to his feet. "Jane," he said, walking toward me with his arms spread wide. He was wearing faded jeans, black Prada boots, the watch I'd given him last Christmas, and a pricey denim shirt distressed to look as if it cost ten dollars or less, though it probably went for a couple hundred.

Ignoring my look of dismay and my rigid stiffness, he hugged me and moved in for a kiss. Grimacing, I turned my head so his lips brushed against my cheek.

"I'm not mad at you anymore," he said.

"Wow. Wish I could say the same. Why don't you please go now."

"I see you made it back safely from Brooklyn."

He waited for my reaction to his little joke, which, sadly for him, was a narrowed-eye look. I removed his hand from the small of my back, walked to my desk, and sat down. "Hugh, why are you here?"

"I'm here because you're my best girl. C'mon, Jane. Give me a break."

Unlikely. It wasn't that my heart was cold, it was that my heart wasn't registering Hugh at all.

"Hugh, I've got a ton of work to do."

Suddenly a little-boy, have-pity-on-me look came over his face. "Jane, I need your help. I don't ask for much."

My eyebrows raised, but he went on anyway.

"Look, let's be honest with one another. I need this movie role. I need *Thank Heaven*. Okay, are you happy now? I'm humbled and I'm humiliated."

I still said nothing, though I got what he was saying and even felt an iota of pity for him. Still, this was the same Hugh who'd wanted to trade an engagement ring for a movie part and who had left me stranded in Brooklyn.

"It's not going to happen, Hugh. I'm sorry, honestly I am. I *am*. But you're not going to get the part. You aren't Michael."

"I am! For God's sake, Jane. I created that character."

"No. *You did not.* You had *nothing* to do with creating Michael. Trust me on that."

His eyes opened wider, and that mean little sneer of his appeared. "You disgusting little shit!" he spat. "Mama's little girl pretending that she's Mama. Still in a fairy-tale world from when you were eight years old."

I stood up behind my desk, expecting my hands to begin trembling, but they didn't. "That was nasty, Hugh, even for you."

"You know where you can shove that little movie of yours? I was doing you a favor, volunteering to be in that piece of sentimental crap! It wouldn't even be getting made if you weren't Vivienne Margaux's very needy daughter."

My eyes were filling with tears, but Hugh didn't seem to notice, and that was the only good thing happening. He came closer to my desk, stabbing his finger at me as he talked. "You need *me*, Jane. I don't need *you*. You need *my* talent. I don't need yours. Which is a good thing. Because you don't *have* any talent."

Everything went red, just like in books, and a burning rage filled my chest. "I wouldn't be so sure," I said. "Watch *this*, Hugh."

I pulled my arm back and punched Hugh in the face, as hard as I could.

Silence.

We were both stunned. Hugh had both hands over his left eye, but his right eye was wide and staring.

A second later, intense pain filled my hand, and I looked down to see if I'd broken any knuckles.

"My God, Jane, have you completely gone out of your mind?"

With my typical luck, my mother had arrived just in time to see me slug Hugh. Excellent. I was sure I'd be able to live this down. Someday. Right after Vivienne finally recovered from the outfit I'd chosen to wear to my sixth-grade graduation, which I was still hearing about occasionally.

"She has!" Hugh sputtered. "She's gone nuts!"

You know, I really couldn't argue with them. I mean, what was I going to say? "I wouldn't have had to hit you if my imaginary friend, possibly boyfriend, had been here"?

I think not.

Fifty-two

MY MOTHER and those damn stilettos of hers had come click-clacking into the room, not to see me, but to make sure I had accepted Hugh's lame-ass apology.

"Jane, *what* is going on?" she asked.

"She's insane, that's what happened!" Hugh cried.

"Nothing, really, Mother," I said calmly. "Hugh and I just formally broke up."

"Broke up?" she asked. "How? Why? What am I missing here? I'm lost, and I never get lost."

"I can see why you might be confused," I said. "But after all, we were never very much of a couple to begin with. More like a solo act with a sidekick."

Wide-eyed, my mother stared at me, then leaned out my office door. "MaryLouise!"

She must have been lurking outside the office door,

listening to the fireworks, because she responded in record time.

"Get me some ice wrapped in a linen towel," Vivienne said.

Leave it to Vivienne to specify the type of material for the towel.

Hugh thanked Vivienne for her concern, and she led him to the three-seater sofa against the wall. "I'm okay," he said. "I'll just sit here a minute. Vivienne, I don't know what I did wrong."

Well, as I said, he's an actor.

My mother turned her attention toward me.

"See that, Jane? What has gotten into you? You can't go around smacking people like Hugh. You could have hurt him."

"She *did* hurt me," came Hugh's muffled voice.

"No more than he's hurt me," I said. "I guess you haven't heard about the wedding proposal debacle."

"Jane, don't be flip. I'm being serious."

"So am I. Or do my feelings not count, because it's only me?"

"Listen, Jane, this isn't your fantasy world, where you can do anything you feel like," Vivienne said.

"Oh, good thing you cleared that up," I said snippily, crossing my arms over my chest.

"I can't imagine anything Hugh could have done to provoke physical violence on your part."

"Really? Well, when you have a few hours, I'll give you the list. As for now, I want the two of you to leave my office."

Vivienne's cheeks flamed, and she walked toward me, stopping inches away from my desk.

"This is not *your* office. This is *my* office. *Every* ashtray, *every* desk, *every* computer, *every* toilet, *every* scrap of paper, *every* Xerox machine..."

My mouth dropped open.

"You wouldn't be working here if it weren't for me. You certainly wouldn't be working here if I knew you were going to physically abuse a talented actor like Hugh McGrath. I don't have to put up with behavior like this."

"You're right, Mother. You don't."

Anger was boiling over inside me. I reached down and grabbed my black leather satchel. Then I swept as much as I could from the top of my desk—papers and letters and pens and photographs—into the bag, making sure I got my Rolodex.

"Don't be ridiculous, Jane."

"Oh, I'm not, Mother. I'm being as sane as I've been in years." Then I added—because I'm me— "I'm sorry."

I walked past her, and I walked past Hugh. And

suddenly I had a crazy thought: *No kiss today, Mother?*

At the door I almost collided with MaryLouise.

As I headed down the hallway toward the elevator I heard her say, "They didn't have a linen towel, Ms. Margaux. You'll have to settle for cotton."

Fifty-three

THAT MORNING, Michael had donned his head-
phones and jogged over to the Olympia Diner to see
Patty, to make sure she was all right, but she wasn't
there. So he sat down, had a big, greasy breakfast,
and tried to make some sense out of everything that
was happening. Like the fact that *he thought he was
falling in love with Jane Margaux.*

He had all the classic symptoms—pounding heart,
sweaty palms, dreamy lapses in attention, a certain
degree of immaturity, happiness in just about every
part of his body. After last night, he had to see Jane
again. Today. Worse, he had to kiss her again. He'd
meet her at her office tonight. He couldn't make
himself stay away, even if it might be the right thing
to do for all concerned.

When he got home from breakfast, he nearly ran

into Patty—and her daughter. They were leaving his building.

What was this? Not good!

Patty was crying, and the little girl looked sad and displaced too. Michael had seen that look many times before with his kids, and it always broke his heart.

"Hi, Patty," he said, then immediately bent down to talk to the little girl. "Hello, sweetheart. Your name is Holly, right? What's going on?"

"My mommy's sad," she said. "She broke up with her boyfriend, Owen."

"Yeah? Your mommy's very strong, though. Tough as nails. Are *you* okay?"

"I guess so. I talked to my friend Martha about it." Then the girl whispered, "She's invisible, you know."

"Ah, I *do* know, actually," Michael said, since Martha was standing right there, looking concerned. She gave him a little wave. "Hi," Michael said, and winked at Holly. "How are you, Martha?"

Martha made a so-so gesture with her hand.

Then Michael stood up. "You're a terrific person, Patty. You know that, right? Owen is a...not-ready-for-grown-ups player," he said. No beating around the bush about that.

"Thank you, Michael. Not your fault," Patty said. "My fault."

Then she picked up Holly and hurried down the front steps, with Martha right behind. "Owen *is* a shit," Martha muttered to Michael as she passed him.

He watched the trio leave, ran up the four flights to his floor. With no plan in mind, he headed for Owen's door, and was about to pound the hell out of it, but stopped himself.

Screw it! Owen Pulaski wasn't worth it and probably never would be. Something had probably happened in his childhood to mess him up—in fact, it had probably happened to a lot of men—but he couldn't fix that, could he? He couldn't fix that little boys weren't allowed to show their emotions, and that seemed unfair to them, and made them as angry as hell, sometimes for the rest of their lives, so that they took it out on everybody, but especially women.

Suddenly the door opened, and Owen was standing there. He looked startled to see Michael, and a guilty expression crossed his face. But he immediately wiped it away and put on a big shit-eating grin.

"Hey, Mike! What's happening, bro?"

So Michael hit him. "I'm *judging* you, Owen. Consider yourself judged."

But then, being Michael, he reached down and helped the big lug up off the floor.

"I'm telling you, Owen. You've got it all wrong. There's nothing better than love in this life. This is a tall order—but find somebody to love you, and try your hardest to love her back, the best you can. And not Patty, or I'll be back."

Having said that, Michael hit the streets again. He needed to see Jane—*now.*

Fifty-four

TWENTY-THREE MINUTES LATER, maybe twenty-five but who was counting, Michael was in an elevator headed up to Jane's office. This couldn't wait. When the doors opened, he could tell that something was wrong. Instead of Elsie's usual welcoming smile, she looked upset.

"I'm going back to see Jane," Michael said.

"She's not here. I was hoping she was with you. Jane walked out of here half an hour ago."

Michael could hear Vivienne talking loudly behind the door. Then he recognized the shrill voice of the bad actor named Hugh. He couldn't understand what they were saying but caught the words "Jane" and "crazy," and they both seemed to be in some kind of panic. "That girl has no idea how much I love her," Vivienne said, "no idea at all."

"What happened to her?" Michael asked Elsie. "Is Jane all right?"

"Well, I'm not sure, but she had a terrible fight with her mother and her boyfriend—"

Michael began to interrupt—he's not her boyfriend!—then he stopped himself.

Elsie continued, "All I know is...Jane stormed out of here, and she said, 'Hold all my calls. Forever!'"

Elsie had barely finished when the door opened and Vivienne and Hugh stepped out. Hugh was holding a towel against his face. Michael hoped someone had hit him. Someone like Jane.

Vivienne's voice was venomous as she spoke to Michael. "*You!* You had something to do with this. Jane has never acted this way before. You corrupted her!" She was wagging her finger at him like a stern schoolteacher at Superficial Academy.

"I don't know what you're talking about," Michael broke in. "Jane is an adult. And she's incorruptible! Unlike Hugh!"

Hugh's eyes narrowed, and suddenly he rushed at Michael and threw a haymaker sort of punch, the kind that would have been choreographed on a stage set. Michael blocked it easily and, without thinking, crunched an uppercut into the pit of Hugh's stomach.

The actor doubled over and then sat down on the floor, more startled than hurt.

And Michael was even more stunned: *two* punches in less than an hour.

"I'm sorry," Michael said, but then he changed his mind. "Well, I'm not. You've been asking for that, Hugh. I'm a little sorry about Owen. I'm glad I hit *you*."

"Elsie, call nine-one-one!" Vivienne yelled, her face red. "Call security! Call somebody! And you!" She snarled at Michael. "You keep away from Jane, and Hugh, and don't you dare come to this office again."

Michael said, "How about two out of three?"

Fifty-five

THE NEXT THING MICHAEL KNEW, he was out on the street again. He experienced the same symptoms he had earlier, but in a more troubling way: anxiety, fear, an uncomfortable pressure on his chest. He had the same questions about Jane, and about himself too. One thing he *didn't* have was Jane's cell phone number. He thought of that as he passed one of the few public telephones left in New York.

There was no point in going to Jane's apartment. If she'd left her office in a fury, she wouldn't go someplace where Vivienne could easily find her. So where would she go?

He kept walking, and when he got tired of walking he began running and when he got tired of running he just ran faster. People gave him a wide berth on the sidewalk, as if he were crazy, and maybe they were right about that. New Yorkers knew crazy.

He slid on his headphones and listened to Corinne Bailey Rae. That helped some. Corinne was a calming influence. Not heading anywhere in particular, he ran up Riverside Drive, and at 110th Street the soaring spires of the Cathedral of St. John the Divine began to fill the sky.

Actually, this street was known as the Cathedral Parkway, and St. John the Divine was the largest cathedral in the world. That was because St. Peter's in Rome wasn't classified as a cathedral. Michael knew about such things. He had always read a lot, considered himself a student.

He pulled open one of the smaller doors that was cut into the huge ones. Then he walked in, knelt, and blessed himself.

The church was enormous, at least a couple hundred yards in length, and suddenly he felt small. He remembered hearing or reading somewhere that the Statue of Liberty would fit comfortably under the central dome. That looked about right.

Michael felt so...*human,* kneeling here in the cathedral. And he wasn't sure if he liked it. But he also wasn't sure that he didn't.

Fifty-six

MICHAEL TURNED OFF the music in his head-phones and began to pray. He wanted answers, needed answers, but none seemed to be coming his way. Finally, he raised his head and looked around the magnificent church. He'd always liked every-thing about the cathedral: the blend of French Gothic and Romanesque styles; the chapels radiating from the ambulatory; the Byzantine columns and arches; voices echoing, an organist practicing somewhere. *God lives here! He must,* Michael thought.

A calm came over him as his eye fell on the mag-nificent Rose Window situated over the altar. His heart quieted some.

Then, to his utter amazement, a tear formed in his eye. It welled up, blurred his vision, and rolled down his cheek.

"What is happening to me?" he whispered. He'd

cut himself shaving, knocked down two guys in the same day (though both had deserved it), and now he was crying. In fact, an overwhelming sadness was overtaking him. *So this is what sorrow feels like. This is the ache in the heart, the catch in the throat,* that he had heard and read so much about.

He'd never felt it before, though, and it was so painful and unpleasant that he wanted it to stop. He snapped his fingers, but nothing happened. He really wasn't in control here, was he? He was lost, floundering, confused. The intense pumping in his heart had been replaced by a small, stabbing hurt, and with the hurt came clarity, a sense of knowledge. A horrible sense of knowledge.

And maybe...a message. Was that what was happening?

Michael thought that he had an answer to his prayers, but he didn't want this to be it. He thought he knew why he was back in New York, and why he'd met up again with Jane Margaux. These feelings, kind of like premonitions, had always preceded his new assignments, and he was having one now. The message was very clear, and he couldn't remember any of the feelings ever being so anguished before. Not once, not ever, as far back as he could remember.

"Oh no," he whispered out loud. "That can't be it."

But it was, wasn't it? It made sense of everything

that had happened up to now. This was the missing piece to the puzzle that he had been trying to solve. It explained why he had found Jane. Of course it did. It was the perfect answer.

He looked up at the glorious Rose Window again. Then at the altar. This couldn't be happening. But clearly it was.

Many years ago Michael had helped guide Jane into this life. He had eased her way, been her imaginary friend until he'd had to leave her when she'd turned nine.

And now he was the one who'd been chosen to bring Jane *out* of life. He understood this now. He got it. This was about human mortality, wasn't it?

Jane was going to die.

That was why he was here in New York.

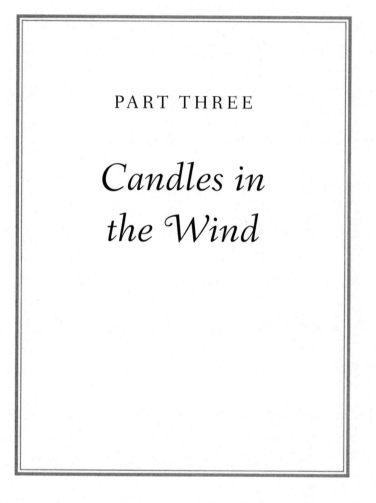

PART THREE

*Candles in
the Wind*

Fifty-seven

CALL IT A MESSAGE, maybe. Or a wake-up call. An instinct?

I felt the need to come to one of our "places": the front steps of the Met, my favorite view in New York since I'd been a little girl and had come here with Michael.

I'd been sitting on the steps for a while. When I had stormed out of my mother's office, I'd automatically told the cabdriver to take me here. Now my anger had faded and transformed itself into something vaguely resembling strength. At least that's what I was telling myself. *What doesn't kill you makes you stronger, right?* I'd never particularly liked that cliché, but I wasn't above using it now.

And every spring flower seemed to be in bloom. From where I sat, I could see pink apple blossoms, azaleas bursting with dynamic red. A gold-and-orange checkerboard of newly planted marigolds filled a garden near Fifth Avenue.

That's better, much better.

Schoolchildren tumbled out of school buses in front of the museum. Old ladies with canes walked carefully up the steps, probably to see the Jackie Kennedy costume exhibit. I'd been there, done that.

A teenage couple sat a few steps away from me. They kissed longingly, and I enjoyed watching them, because for this moment, at least, they were hopelessly in love. *Was I in love too, and was it hopeless?*

The good news was that I felt like a huge weight had been lifted from my shoulders. I was free of Vivienne, free of Hugh, free of the pressures of my job, free of nine to five (or, rather, nine to nine), free of worrying about whether I looked good or bad. At least for the next hour or so.

I wanted one thing in my life: Michael. I knew his presence was unreliable, and that it wasn't entirely in his control. I knew he might disappear on me one day, and probably would. But love takes chances, and I wanted to take a chance right now. For once in my life, I knew what I wanted.

That was a start, wasn't it?

I heard a voice, and I looked up and had to shade
my eyes from the glare of the sun.

"Excuse me, miss. Is this step taken?"

It was Michael.

"How do you know I'm a miss?" I asked.

Fifty-eight

IT REALLY WAS MICHAEL. He'd found me.
But, God, did he look like crap!

"What happened to you?" I asked, after I'd given
him the once-over.

"What do you mean? What's the matter with
me?"

"You look like you haven't slept in days. Your eyes
are all bloodshot. Your clothes are wringing wet with
perspiration. You're..."

He sat next to me and held my hand. "I'm fine,
Jane. I'm really fine." He leaned in and kissed my
neck. Gentle, strong. I didn't know which, and I didn't
care. Then Michael kissed me on the lips, and every
nerve inside me lit up. He kissed me a second time.
And a third. I stared into his eyes and felt my whole
body start tingling.

"Why aren't you at work?" he asked.

With great effort, I concentrated on what he'd just said.

I could tell that he was wise to what had happened. "Jane?"

"Why aren't I at work? Because I punched the crap out of Hugh McGrath? I think I bruised my knuckles, too." Michael kissed my hands.

"Because, for once, I told my mother where to stick it, and it felt just great, Michael. Because I quit my day job, which also happened to be my *night* job most of the time."

Michael gave me a loving smile. "Hooray for Jane! Good for you!"

I laughed. "Hooray for Jane? Good for me? I hope this doesn't mean you think your work is done here. Because it *isn't,* not even close."

"You are an endless project," he said with another smile. "Changing, evolving, surprising."

"Excellent sentence fragment. You've been practicing."

Then I leaned over and kissed him again. "I've decided I'm done with being miserable and oppressed. I want to actually enjoy life. I want to have fun. Doesn't everyone deserve that?" I asked.

"Absolutely," he said. "And you most of all."

Suddenly he looked very serious, and his eyes avoided mine.

Uh-oh. "What?" I said.

"Jane, do you remember that time when you were little—and your dad took you for that long spring weekend in Nantucket? Remember that?"

"It was to make up for not taking me anywhere for my fifth birthday. Or my fourth. Probably my third, too."

"Yeah, it was."

"It was the first time I ever remember being really happy," I said, smiling at the distant memory. "You and I built sand castles with my stupid Barbie doll pail and matching shovel. We went to some ice cream place in town where they mixed chocolate chips and peanuts right into the coffee ice cream. We went swimming every day, even though the water was freezing, with a capital Brrr."

"Good times, huh?" Michael asked.

"The best. Remember the Cliffside Beach Club? And Jetties Beach?"

"Let's go back there, Jane."

I smiled. "I'd love to. When?"

"Right now. Today. Let's go. What do you say?"

I stared into Michael's green eyes and I sensed that something was up, but I didn't want to ask him what it was. I figured that he'd tell me soon enough. Plus, there was chicken Jane again. The fantasy is much better than the reality.

"I'd love to go to Nantucket," I said. "But you have to promise to answer a few questions while we're there."

Fifty-nine

"FIRST QUESTION," Jane said on the ride out to the airport. "You weaseled out of telling me if you ever dated. But have you ever fallen in love?"

Michael made a face, sighed, then said, "The way it works, Jane, is that after a while, I seem to forget what happened in the past. That's not my choice, by the way. In answer to your question, *I don't think so.*"

"So this would be the first?" asked Jane, and Michael smiled at her confidence in assuming that he had fallen in love with her. He hadn't said so, but she'd been able to tell. And she wasn't wrong.

"How about sex?" she asked next.

Michael started to laugh. "Let's ease our way into this. One question at a time, okay? Now, let's talk about something else, Jane-Sweetie."

"Okay. When I was a wee, small, little girl, I remember that we used to take Eastern Airlines up to Cape Cod. We'd go a couple of times every summer," Jane said as the cab rattled up to the old Marine Terminal at LaGuardia Airport.

Michael gave her a kiss, lingering on the softness of her lips and noticing the twinkle in her eyes. She was a grown-up woman, but he loved the innocent, childlike quality she still had.

"Are you trying to shut me up?" Jane asked. "This kissing thing?"

"Not at all. I just ... like it." And he kissed Jane again.

The cabdriver finally barked back at them, "You two gonna get out of the cab, or are you going to sit here and make lovey-dovey all day?"

"Lovey-dovey," Jane told the guy, laughing, and he almost smiled back.

Michael paid the driver and grabbed their two small suitcases. Once inside the old terminal, he paused and peered around.

"What are you looking for now?"

"Him."

Michael pointed to an old guy in a floppy brown windbreaker with the letters CCPA on the chest pocket. His face was sunburned and covered with age lines.

"Cape Cod Private Air?" Michael asked as he walked up to him.

"The one and only," he answered in a gravelly voice. "Follow me, folks. You're Jane and Michael, right?"

"That would be us," said Jane.

They followed the old man, and in a few minutes they were boarding a small plane that looked suspiciously like the one Michael had seen in pictures of Lindbergh's transatlantic flight.

"You think this plane'll make it to Nantucket?" Jane asked, only half joking. Michael hoped she wasn't remembering any recent crashes of small planes.

"Have a little faith, lady," the pilot said.

"We've got plenty of that," said Michael. "You have no idea."

In a few minutes, the propellers were spinning, and the plane was cruising down the runway like a drunk stumbling around the Bowery.

"When I imagined my own death, I hadn't actually pictured a plane crash." Jane tried to joke, but her hand gripped Michael's firmly.

Michael felt his throat tighten and his chest start to hurt again. Jane was being funny, but he'd gotten a bad feeling about what she had just said. Were they meant to crash, and then, what, he would die too? After all, he had experienced a number of firsts lately. Was death to be the last first for him, as it was for everyone?

"We're not going to crash, Jane," he said, and held her hand more tightly.

Sixty

THE PLANE TOOK OFF, taking its sweet time finding its cruising altitude. In Michael's opinion they were spending way too much time examining the rooftops of Queens. Even when they had moved up among the clouds, the plane made a putt-putt-putt sound that wasn't exactly reassuring.

Somehow, though, in about fifty minutes they were closing in on Nantucket. They could see miles of sandy shoreline down below, plus a few smaller islands. Then they landed—without a hitch. Jane finally let go of Michael's hand.

Even though it was only late spring, the place was crowded with people in summer-bright clothing. A sea of pinks and yellows and lime greens. Carefully distressed jeans and surfing jams. Seagulls squawking overhead as if they'd never seen tourists before, or maybe they'd seen far too many of them.

Michael and Jane made their way to the taxi line. The sun was sharp overhead. The air was crisp and clean.

As they waited, Jane reached up to Michael's face and held it in both her hands. "Michael, where are you?" she asked.

"What? I'm right here."

He didn't know what to say, but knew he'd better pull himself together. He'd been thinking about Jane dying, but she was right here, wasn't she? They both were. So why was he wasting precious time? Why did anybody? Why waste a second of the time that you have? It was so obvious to him now.

"We're together," Jane said, looking into his eyes. "Let's just enjoy this time, okay? Just put aside everything on your mind and be with me. Let's take everything one day at a time. An hour at a time. Minute by minute. Okay?"

Michael covered one of her hands with his and turned his head to kiss her palm gently. He smiled and nodded.

"Yes," he said. "Minute by minute. Hour at a time. Day at a time." Cabs and jitneys kept pulling up to the little airport. People would load them up with canvas bags from L. L. Bean and shopping bags from Dean and DeLuca. Michael and Jane waited with growing impatience. Finally, they were at the head of the line.

"Throw those valises in the trunk," the cabdriver said.

Valises. What a wonderful old-fashioned word to use. Hearing it made Michael smile, and seeing him smile made Jane laugh. "Good. You're back."

"I'm right here, Jane. That's my hand holding your hand. That's my fast-beating heart you can hear."

Jane smiled, then took one last look around. Collecting memories, Michael thought. The tall sea grass bent in the wind. Gulls flew overhead. A blond teenage girl had set up a makeshift stand near the taxi line to sell homemade jams.

The cabdriver could have been the brother of the pilot who had just flown them up. A down-home, no-nonsense New Englander, aged somewhere between sixty and eighty-five.

"Now, where can I take you nice folks?" he asked.

"The India Street Inn," Michael said.

"Good choice," he responded. "Old whaling captain's house, y'know."

Jane smiled and squeezed Michael's hand tighter.

"Good choice," she repeated. "Love them whaling captains."

"And *yes,*" Michael suddenly said into her ear, "in answer to your question a while back. *Yes,* I have had sex before."

Sixty-one

HERE'S WHAT JANE AND MICHAEL didn't see driving into town: fast-food restaurants, souvenir stores, even a traffic signal. This actually *was* paradise. They did see a couple of homemade signs advertising the tenth Nantucket Wine Festival and the thirty-fifth Figawi Boat Race. A perfect beginning to their visit.

Then their cab pulled up in front of the India Street Inn.

"This is what a Nantucket bed-and-breakfast should look like," Jane said as they walked through the front door. That had been Michael's plan: something simple and beautiful, not overdone, just pretty and fresh and right for their trip.

They certainly had it down to a fine science at this place, Michael thought: red geraniums in royal blue window flower boxes, colorful geometric quilts on the wall, sleigh-riding prints in the hallways, and, of course the crusty old New England woman who ran the place.

"You got a reservation? If not, we don't have a room for you," she said. "As in: no room at the India Street Inn."

Michael gave her the name "Michaels," and moments later they were sent to suite 21 on the second floor. There was one big room with a queen-size bed and lots of country pine antiques, a hand-painted mural on the wall, and fluffy white towels everywhere. A door from the bathroom led to another smaller bedroom. *Connecting bedrooms.* What Michael had asked for when he called.

"This is great" was all Jane said as she checked everything out.

She walked to the window in the larger bedroom and opened it wide. A cool breeze blew her hair back, and Michael thought she had never looked more beautiful. Could anything be more special than being here with Jane? He didn't think so. Certainly no one had ever made his heart beat fast like this. He would remember if it had happened before, wouldn't he?

Jane picked up a brochure from the desk, and she began reading, "Coffee in the front parlor starting at six in the morning. Windsurfing lessons on the far bay every Monday and Thursday. You can rent bikes. Also, visitors can go up in the tower of the Old North Church. Can we? I want to do everything. Okay?"

Michael could almost feel Jane's happiness in the way she spoke. She wasn't acting like a little girl, but she had the same wonderful qualities—enthusiasm, curiosity, innocence.

I love her, he thought, and said, "Okay. Anything you want."

And he decided to leave it at that very good place for the moment.

Sixty-two

THE INNKEEPER GAVE THEM two old Schwinn bikes—nothing fancy, thick tires, rusted paint, pedal brakes, many creaking parts. She pointed them in the general direction of Siasconset, saying, "Most tourists think 'Sconset's real pretty, and special. Because it *is* real pretty and special."

Jane took off first, and Michael followed along on the Milestone Road. There wasn't much traffic—an occasional Jeep; a motorbike; a fish delivery truck; a big, vulgar, taxi-yellow Hummer—then a bunch of kids on racing bikes, moving faster than some of the cars.

"Have a great honeymoon!" one of the kids shouted at them. Michael and Jane looked at each other and smiled. After four or five miles, they came upon a split-rail fence and a vista that looked amazingly like the Serengeti in Africa. Next they passed

Tom Nevers Road and a grand view across cran-
berry bogs. Then came the Nantucket Golf Club,
acres of rolling, manicured fairways and greens that
actually made golf look like it might be fun.

Another hill came, higher than the rest. A wooden
sign in the shape of an arrow said: SIASCONSET. They
crested down, and there it was: a white beach that
stretched out to the ocean. Michael wondered if Jane
had known that a deep red afternoon sun would
just be moving overhead, ready to set, ready to cast
beautiful light down on them.

"Tell me you've ever seen anything this sweet
before," she said as they settled on the sand.

"Actually, I have." He was looking into her eyes.

"Stop!" she said, laughing and blushing. "You're
going to lose all credibility, on our first day here."

"Okay."

"No, don't stop."

So he put his arm around her and watched her
from the corner of his eye and lived in the moment.

I just love Jane. That's all there is for now.

Sixty-three

ABOUT THAT SEX THING: It didn't happen our
first night on Nantucket, and I tried not to overthink
it, and failed. Or to let it bother me at all, and failed
a second time, pretty miserably.

Early the next morning, we headed off to what
was supposedly the highest point on the island,
called Folger Hill. We even had the good sense
to slather ourselves with sunblock and wear long-
sleeved shirts. I was loving this, every minute of it,
every second. Despite not knowing what would
come next, despite all the questions I still had, I was
taking my own advice and just relishing everything,
day by day, hour by hour, minute by minute.

The ride on Polpis Road seemed long. Maybe I
was just tired. Plus, it was overcast, the kind of foggy
day that delayed the ferries and kept the supply
boats from coming in on time.

Eventually, we made it to a small harbor town called Madaket. There was a bait store, a hardware store, and a gathering spot called Smith's Point. At about 11:30, we ate fish and chips at a broken-down shack that we first thought had been abandoned.

"How'd you know about this place?" I asked.

"I'm not sure. I just knew, Jane."

Maybe to shut me up, Michael kissed me, which I never seemed to tire of, and then we ate the crispiest, most delicious deep-fried pieces of fish. The cook had wrapped them in pages of the *Inquirer and Mirror* newspaper. We doused the cod with malt vinegar. And because Michael believed you can never have enough fried foods at one sitting, we ordered a rolled newspaper cone of French fries, also doused with vinegar. Meanwhile, old Bob Dylan songs were playing from the open-air kitchen, and everything seemed so perfect and magical that I felt like crying.

Sometimes I would catch Michael looking off toward the roiling sea. When he did, he seemed to be drifting away again. I wanted to know where it was he was going, what he was thinking. Did he already know when he would leave me? I shut my eyes, unwilling to think about it. I wouldn't think about it till it happened.

And it had to happen, right? That was how this

had to end. Michael would leave to take care of a child somewhere, maybe not even in New York.

It was inevitable, so I put the sad thought right out of my mind, and stayed on vacation, stayed in love with him.

"What do you remember about me as a little girl?" I asked, and sat back, and listened to Michael's memories for an hour or so. Interestingly, he seemed to remember *everything* now, even the coffee ice cream with rivers of hot fudge.

Sixty-four

"I NEVER THOUGHT I would say the words I am about to say," I said.

"And those words are?"

"I'm too full to eat dinner."

"Jane, we haven't eaten anything since lunch."

"You eat, I'll just watch," I said, and Michael looked at me, concerned.

Back at the India Street Inn, we showered and changed into jeans and T-shirts and windbreakers. Then we walked. That was us: walking and talking. We went away from the town center, away from the shops, away from worries, responsibilities, anything that had to do with the so-called real world, my job, Vivienne.

We walked past three-hundred-year-old houses, where sailors and whalers once lived, where patient, faithful wives waited for their husbands to come home from the sea; houses that had stood here long before the media celebrities, pop singers, actors, and authors had descended on the island.

We passed a windmill, lots of little ponds, walking tracks, and more "trophy" houses than you could throw a seashell at.

"Sure you're not hungry?" Michael asked as we made our way back to the inn.

"There are only two things I'm sure of," I said. "One, I'm not hungry, and two…" I paused, not for effect, but because I wanted to be sure about what I was about to say.

"Go on," he said. "Two things you're sure of, and the second is?"

"Two, I love you, Michael. I think I've loved you my entire life. I needed to say that out loud, not just inside my head."

We stopped walking, and Michael held me by the hips and then moved his hands up my back, exciting me in a way that made me, well, up for just about anything. We kissed again, and he did that bear-hug-lifting thing that I loved, and then we walked the short distance back to the inn. I felt as if there was a neon sign glaring in the front window: NOW WHAT?

Sixty-five

"ALMOST DIDN'T RECOGNIZE you two without a bike between your legs," the lady innkeeper said as we walked through the front door. I glanced at her, startled. I don't think she meant it to sound the way it did because she clammed right up.

Michael and I laughed, then walked up to our room, holding hands, but quietly, not a word spoken between us for a change. I didn't even have a question I wanted to ask him right now.

Inside the bedroom we started kissing again. The kisses were hard, and then soft, soft and then hard, soft, brushing our lips against each other's, listening to each other breathe. How far will this go? I wondered. How far *can* it go?

"Your place or mine?" I finally managed a few words.

"I . . . I," Michael muttered, and he had a concerned look on his face.

"I'll take that as an 'aye, aye,' " I said, and grinned. He looked solemnly into my eyes.

"Michael, c'mon," I said as I gently stroked the back of his neck and pressed myself against him. "This is good. This *will* be good. I swear. I promise. I hope? I think so."

He smiled then and took my hand, leading me into the smaller bedroom. "This will be good," he muttered softly. "Has to be. It's all been leading here, to this moment. And here we are. Are you okay?"

I smiled again. "You had me at 'aye, aye.' "

Sixty-six

I WAS BOTH EAGER AND NERVOUS. Mostly eager, but... "This is always the worst part," I said, sitting down on the edge of his bed.

"What is?"

"Taking my clothes off."

"Maybe for you," Michael said teasingly. "For me, seeing you take your clothes off will definitely be the highlight of the last several years."

I started fiddling with the buttons on my blouse, and I suddenly had one of those weird, inconsequential concerns that always seemed to strike when I desperately needed to be focusing on something else. But here was a question for any ministers, priests, or rabbis out there: Is it all right to make love with your imaginary friend? Surely something filled with this much love couldn't be a sin. But if it inexplicably was a sin, was it major or minor? Mortal or venial? What if your friend is an angel, or might be, but doesn't know for sure himself?

Whatever it was, Michael saw my hesitation and took matters, and my blouse, into his own hands. He was pretty skillful at unhooking my bra—one-handed, and in less than five seconds.

"You're good," I said, feeling nerves fluttering in my stomach. I felt a blush rising on my neck and face.

"You haven't seen anything yet," he said, giving me a warm look.

"Oh, I hope so."

"Me too."

We started to kiss again, and then Michael cupped my breasts in his hands, making me whimper in a way that would be totally embarrassing under any other circumstances. In this case, I have to say, it sounded kind of hot. He held me gently, as if afraid of hurting me, and softly rubbed his thumbs over my nipples, making me shiver. Gentle, sweet, as nice as could be. Next, he traced my stomach with his fingertips. I liked that too and felt myself melting under his touch.

He had a beautiful touch. Sublime. Maybe he *was* an angel? At this point, I neither knew nor cared. The little hairs on my body were all standing on end, standing at attention, whatever happens at exquisite times like this. I had no idea: I'd never done *exquisite* before.

"I love the way you touch me," I whispered against his cheek. "No one's ever touched me like this."

His breathing was getting rough, and he paused in kissing to say, "Me too."

He tugged me down on top of him. Then his tongue licked lightly at my nipples, and my breath left me in a whoosh. I stopped thinking about whether Michael was experienced at this or not. We were together, and I just loved being with him. Maybe because I could tell that Michael was happy to be with me too. I could feel it in his touch, and I could see it in his green eyes. He was loving this as much as I was.

I kissed him again, tasted the sweetness of his mouth, then pulled my face away. I looked into his eyes and whispered, "Okay, yes, please."

"Okay, Jane, yes, thank you," Michael said, and smiled like the sun rising. Then he rolled me onto my back, and I was opening up for him and feeling his delicious weight on me, the heat of his skin. Then he was inside me, and this had to be the right thing to do, it just had to be, because Michael said, "I love you so much, Jane. I always have, and I always will."

And that was exactly what I was thinking too, almost word for word.

Sixty-seven

THEY WERE TOGETHER for a long time that night, and Jane slept like a baby afterward, but Michael couldn't. He lay in bed with his face inches from hers, and stroked her hair for what must have been an hour or more.

Looking at her lying there so peacefully made him want to... *break all the windows in the room.* Life was unfair, he understood that, for the first time, really. Was that why he was here, so that he could learn to be more compassionate? If so, this sucked big-time, because he was already pretty damn compassionate. Anyone who was an imaginary friend to a child would have to be. So now who was he supposed to be in this little melodrama? An angel? An ordinary person? An imaginary friend? He had as many questions as Jane did, and no one was giving answers to either of them.

He quietly swung around, sitting up on the side of the bed. He walked into the bathroom and looked into the mirror.

You've got to tell Jane what's going on, what's going to happen to her.

But he wasn't sure if that was the right thing to do. It could be the wrong thing. He turned on the shower, as hot as he could stand it. The shower shelf was filled with Jane's things—almond soap, Kiehl's conditioner, shampoo.

How sick was she? Was it cancer? Something to do with her heart? Yesterday, after the fish and chips, Jane had said she was so full that she wished she could call a cab and not have to bike back to the inn. Then she was tired on the walk through the village. And she wasn't eating much, not by normal Jane standards.

"Hey, there's so much steam in here, I thought the bathroom was on fire."

He heard her in the room, and he started to smile.

"Michael? Are you in here?" she called out.

"No, he's not here. I'm just a guy with his voice."

Jane laughed as she pushed aside the shower curtain. "*Oh!* And here's something else of Michael's. My God, it's large. And it's growing. Somebody step on it. Hit it with a stick. Or...okay...I guess you could do *that* with it."

Sixty-eight

AND HERE'S WHAT HAPPENED NEXT.

They made love again, then slept again. In the
morning they woke up with smiles on their faces,
and a newfound, joyous sense of wonder and con-
tentment. After breakfast, they went on a chartered
whale-watching trip. Michael loved Jane's excited
amazement when they actually saw a humpback
breech, impossibly close to the boat. After lunch,
they went to the Brant Point Lighthouse. That was
followed by a long walk on the beach, hand in hand,
talking and not talking.

Michael told Jane how long he'd been a "friend,"
and he told her as much as he could remember. He
could recall only the past few assignments; he had
a sense that there had been others, but the memories had faded, like dreams. Seeing Jane now, as a
grown-up, his memory of their earlier years came

back. He honestly didn't know if every kid had an invisible friend, but he hoped so.

That night Michael called a local restaurant, and a taxi delivered lobster, steamers, and corn on the cob to them right on the beach. They went back to the inn, and made love again, and got even more comfortable with each other. And the sex was great, better than Michael could have imagined. Probably because they were so in love, and knew each other so well. Jane felt a little queasy during the night, but she was sure it was something that she ate, probably the steamers.

Which led to the next morning, and renting a Sailfish, and then they were on a fishing boat. Jane caught about a dozen bluefish, while Michael caught none. He tried to memorize the way she looked, so delighted and triumphant, pulling in yet another flashing, wiggling bluefish. Her hair shone in the sun, her smile lit the sky. He couldn't wait to go back to the inn with her.

Before dinner, they made love again, with a fierceness that took them both by surprise. Afterward they didn't talk about it, but got on the old bikes and pedaled back to picturesque Siasconset. On the way back to the inn, they stopped and picked armfuls of spicy-scented wild roses, which they put in their wicker bicycle baskets. They had dinner at

Ozzie and Ed's restaurant in town, where Ozzie and Ed practically adopted the two of them and kept calling them "adorable."

On the way back from dinner, Michael said, "Have I ever told you about Kevin Uxbridge?"

"No. Was he one of your children? Your friends?"

"No. Kevin Uxbridge was part of the Douwd race, on *Star Trek*."

"The original or *Next Generation*?"

"*Next Generation*. He met a woman named Rishon and fell in love with her so deeply that he decided to put aside his extraordinary powers to marry her and live a 'mortal life.'"

"I hope it worked out for them," Jane said. "I see a parallel here."

"Well, actually, it didn't work out that well," Michael admitted. "Husnocks came and attacked their colony. Rishon was killed. Kevin Uxbridge was so furious and devastated that he destroyed the Husnock race completely, all fifty billion of them."

"Gosh," said Jane, "that seems a little excessive. But wait, are you Kevin, or am I Kevin?"

"Neither of us is Kevin," Michael said, sounding almost testy.

"O-kaay," said Jane, taking his hand again. "Personally, I always liked the tribbles best."

Michael decided to drop it.

Meanwhile, every time Jane coughed, or looked the least bit weary, it slapped Michael back to reality. Every time she mentioned a leg cramp or her loss of appetite, he felt a shudder. But he couldn't tell her...because...what would it accomplish other than to make these special moments into something terrible, too sad for words?

Sixty-nine

WHEN NIGHT COMES TO NANTUCKET, it can get much more pitch-black than it ever gets in New York City, especially if there's a cloud cover. No moon, no streetlights, no noisy tourists navigating the brick roadways. Jane slept, and Michael stared out the window of their room. In the darkness he could barely see the nearby buildings.

How incredible meeting up with Jane again had been, getting to know her as a woman. And then the feelings growing between them, the dinners and talks, the laughter that could be convulsive at times. The nervous, tentative kisses that were almost like teases, then the passionate ones, where they joined together, heart and soul. And finally, lovemaking, holding Jane for hours, trying to imagine a future for the two of them that went beyond Nantucket.

At about 4:00 that morning, Michael sat at the edge of the bed, watching Jane sleep again, trying to come up with a plan, anything at all. Something must have told her he was up.

"What's the matter, Michael?" she asked in a soft, sleepy voice. "What's happening? Is something the matter? Are you sick?"

"Nothing, Jane. I don't get sick, remember? Go back to sleep. It's four o'clock."

"Come lie down with me. *It's four o'clock.*"

So Michael lay down with Jane, snuggling with her, until she slept again. He watched over her until his eyes stung. He would do anything in his power to save her. Even if it meant...the unthinkable.

Maybe *that* was it. He had a thought, an idea, a nugget of one, anyway. He found the logic of it hopeful. He was there to lead Jane out of this world, correct? That was his mission. But what if he wasn't there anymore?

Pain stabbed through his heart as he pictured his grim, black-and-white, Jane-less existence. But it would be worth it, if she could live. If he wasn't here to help her leave the world, wouldn't she necessarily stay in it? Maybe?

He didn't know. But at this moment, it was all he had.

Still trying to think his idea through, maybe

grasping at straws, he began to throw things into his canvas bag, and then he shut the window so Jane wouldn't catch a chill. He stared at her again. *Am I doing the right thing, leaving her now?*

Will this work? It might. It has to. Jane can't die.

He wanted to kiss her good-bye, to hold her one more time, to talk to her, hear her voice. But he didn't dare wake her. How could he leave her again? Maybe because he had no other idea, and therefore, no choice. "I love you, Jane," he whispered. "I'll love you forever."

Carefully, he closed the door behind him, hurried along the hallway and down the stairs. There was a 5:30 AM ferry to Boston. He made a stop at the front desk and spoke to the night clerk. "My friend is up in suite twenty-one. Can someone check on her in the morning? Tell her I had to leave suddenly. A...friend is sick. Make sure to tell her it's a *friend*. A child."

Michael walked through dark Nantucket streets, which were completely empty. He felt alone, isolated and adrift. He was having trouble just catching his breath, which was unusual. His legs felt incredibly heavy. Finally, tears began to roll down his cheeks. Real tears. Among his first ever.

He pulled his windbreaker tight and waited at the dock. The boat would arrive in about half an hour.

There was already a trace of sunlight on the horizon. Could that mean there was hope?

There had to be, because Jane couldn't die. It was too heartbreaking even to imagine.

Jane can't die now.

Seventy

I WOKE THE NEXT MORNING already smiling, stretching luxuriously, feeling intensely sated in that happy, secure, slightly dragged-through-a-hedge-backward kind of way that comes from making lots of love—making actual love, as opposed to having sex.

I felt wonderful. Sunlight was pouring into the room, as if the sun were trying to shine brighter, just for us. Turning, I was disappointed not to see Michael right beside me. That stupid little travel clock on the wobbly nightstand said 8:55. No way was it that late, though.

What had Michael and I planned to do this morning anyway? Let's see, we'd talked about going back to an antiques store that had some kind of whale-tooth carving Michael liked. But first, breakfast at the coffee shop in town that specialized in blueberry pancakes, although I still wasn't hungry. Maybe because I was shedding some weight and liking the feeling of my body. Or, more likely, because I was in love.

Well, *whatever,* we were going to be late, weren't we? Any day we spent together wasn't long enough. We had to seize every minute. Plus, Michael loved to eat, probably because he never put on an ounce. The creep.

I was just about to jump out of bed when I had a flashback to the night before. My mind wandered to a conversation that Michael had wanted to have, something he needed to tell me. I remembered waking up during the night, and Michael lying down with me.

Where was he?

"Michael?" I called, and got no answer. "Michael, are you there? Michael? Mikey? Mike? Hey, *you!*"

I got out of bed, pushed the hair out of my eyes, and looked around. No Michael. Michael wasn't anywhere.

I was stunned. I couldn't believe it. I glanced around for a note but saw none.

Dumbstruck, I put my hand to my mouth. *He just couldn't have.*

Somehow I stumbled back to my room, where the wrecked bedsheets seemed to mock me. The idea that Michael would literally love me and leave me had never occurred to me. I didn't know whether to feel worried or furious or just painfully, heartbreakingly agonized.

"Michael," I whispered in the empty room. "Michael, how could you? Didn't you love me? You were the one person who did..." *Oh my God, that was it, wasn't it?* What he had wanted to tell me, why he hadn't been able to sleep.

He'd left me again for another child, right? He was back being somebody else's imaginary friend.

I ran around the two bedrooms like a crazy person in search of a lost shred of sanity. All of his stuff was gone. His duffel bag—gone. I pulled out bureau drawers, threw open closet doors. Nothing of Michael's was anywhere. No signs that he'd even been here.

I looked out the window at a day as bright and pretty as any we'd had so far in Nantucket. A perfect day for bike riding and antiques shopping, supper at Ozzie and Ed's, being with someone you loved more than life itself.

"Oh, Michael," I said, "how could you leave me all alone? Again."

This time I wouldn't forget him, because I couldn't ever forgive him—*for breaking my heart twice.*

Seventy-one

MEN SUCK! Even imaginary ones.

I arrived in New York that day, and I felt like
a stranger in my own home; everything in every
room looked as though it belonged to someone else.
Someone who wasn't me. Was this my furniture?
Had I selected the paintings on the wall? Who had
picked out the drapes? Oh, wait. There was a reason
it felt like someone else's apartment. Like Vivienne's
apartment, for example.

And *who* was that in the hallway mirror. It wasn't
just the dark smudges under my eyes that threw me.
I was so thin!

I lugged my *valise* into the bedroom and sat on
the bed. My bleary eyes focused on the nightstand.
The gardenias Michael had given me were gone. My
housekeeper must have tossed the dead blossoms.

Fresh tears welled in my eyes—and I'd thought I was all cried out.

Not even close, Jane-Sweetie!

Suddenly a horrible wave of nausea overwhelmed me. It invaded my stomach and chest, a burning, awful feeling. I barely made it to the bathroom, then knelt at the toilet, throwing up Nantucket's finest shellfish and clutching my stomach. Finally, the wave subsided and I washed my face in the sink. My hands were still shaking, and I looked pale and faintly green in the mirror. Food poisoning. Just what I needed.

When I felt up to it, I checked my messages, hoping against hope that Michael had left some word, some kind of explanation. But first, of course, there was my mother: *"Jane-Sweetie, I'm worried about you. Seriously worried. Please call. Your mother."*

Actually, I suddenly felt as if I did need to call Vivienne. Even though she would be apoplectic about my absence. In fact—and I really mean this—I was surprised she hadn't sent out detectives looking for me.

I tapped Vivienne's number on speed dial. It wasn't answered by either her houseman or her maid and instead went to her outgoing voicemail message.

"You have reached Vivienne Margaux..."

As my mother spoke, I rehearsed the message I was going to leave. I heard the beep.

And then I completely fell apart, and my rehearsed speech fled.

"Mom, it's me. It's Jane. Listen. Michael's left me. Please call me. I love you."

I actually *needed* one of my mother's kisses right now. More than I ever had in my life.

I couldn't speak after that, so I hung up the phone and lay facedown on my bed. Suddenly I was sobbing again, but also coughing, and my throat hurt.

There was no fighting the next bout of nausea. I stumbled into the bathroom and retched horribly. The nausea finally ended. But the coughing wouldn't stop. I tried swallowing hard, but that only made it worse.

The nausea swept over me again, scaring me now. It was burning and blistering inside. There was nothing left to throw up. Just dry heaves. And cold sweats. I collapsed onto the bathroom floor and rested my head on the throw rug. I was burning up and shaking with chills at the same time. I felt like death. The best I could do was to blink my eyes.

I could hear the phone ringing in my bedroom, but I didn't think I was strong enough to stand, or even crawl, to answer it. It had to be Vivienne, though, and I wanted to talk to her.

Or maybe it was Michael?

I pushed myself up off the floor, and I started to hobble.

Seventy-two

MICHAEL'S WORRY, his anxiety, his guilt, his lack of sleep, finally caught up with him on the 5:30 ferry ride from Nantucket to the mainland. His eyes had started to burn again, and his cable-knit sweater wasn't much protection against the damp morning chill blowing off the Atlantic.

His terrible state of worry and confusion continued on the bus ride to the airport in Boston and then on the shuttle from Logan to LaGuardia, and the condition had a strange effect on his vision. It was as if everything he saw was drained of color; most things looked a sickening shade of gray; those that did have a tinge of color were washed-out and weak. Only hours ago he had been in Nantucket, where he'd been incredibly happy with Jane. The happiest he'd ever been in his life. Now everything was changed.

* * *

HE ARRIVED at his apartment building and trudged upstairs. He heard laughter coming from inside Owen's apartment. A woman's voice. Another conquest? My God, was that what Jane would think she had been to him? Would it seem like that to her? Of course it would.

He dropped his bag inside his apartment, but he couldn't stay there. Not right now, not in this state.

Minutes later, he was walking up Broadway fast, watching gray people, gray cabs, and grayer-than-gray New York City buildings. He missed Jane with an ache that felt life-threatening, a terrible pain deep in his chest. He wondered what she was doing, if she was okay. Had his plan worked?

Finally he couldn't bear it anymore: He called her apartment. After listening to the phone ring several times, he heard Jane's voice. *"This is Jane. Please leave a message. It's important to me. Thanks."*

God, he loved her voice.

Near Lincoln Center he barely avoided being hit by a motorcycle that was making a perfectly legal right turn. "Wake the fuck up, asshole!" the driver shouted. Good advice. He would love to wake up out of this horrible nightmare.

He walked another block, determined to keep moving, and suddenly it struck him: *I'm going somewhere, headed to a specific place!*

But where?

Northeast, it seemed.

At last he realized that some outside force was making him move. And then he *knew,* at least he thought he did.

Now he was running.

His eyes filled with tears, and then the tears wouldn't stop. People were staring, and a few offered their help. Michael kept running. He definitely knew where he was going now.

New York Hospital.

And he knew what he was going to find there.

"Oh God, Jane! Don't let this be happening."

I wish, Michael thought, *that I had kissed and hugged Jane more.*

I wish that I had stayed on Nantucket.

I wish—

Seventy-three

YORK AVENUE AND 68TH STREET, finally.
Michael was almost there.

He burst through the front doors of New York
Hospital. Ironically, he'd been to this unfortunate
place before, when Jane had her tonsils out as a
kid. He went right past the front desk, remembering
where the elevators were.

Down the long hallway, to the right.

He was supposed to go to the seventh floor.

Room 703.

Ahead of him, people streamed into the elevator.
Two nurses with their hands linked, a doctor, some
visitors, a little girl who was crying for her grand-
father. Why was all this suffering permitted to happen? Suddenly he was filled with questions.

"I don't think we can squeeze anyone else in
here," a doctor said to him.

"Sorry," he said. "We can squeeze, we can fit. You'd be amazed what we're capable of."

We, he'd thought, and said. *We.*

The people in the elevator exchanged glances, the kind of nervous looks that seemed to say: *We've got a crazy on board.*

The doors finally closed, and the car began to move upward.

"I shouldn't have left her," Michael muttered to himself. *I should have stayed with Jane no matter what. And now look what's happened. His foolish plan hadn't worked. He'd caused her pain for no reason. He'd been so stupid!*

The elevator finally arrived at the seventh floor. Michael pushed out first, then raced past the nurses' desk. He slowed down as he approached room 703.

The door was open a crack. He pushed his sweaty hair back against his head and wiped his face on his sleeve. He needed to look calm and in control. But he wasn't calm. His heart felt as if it might blow apart. He'd never felt tightness in his chest before, and now it was pretty extreme.

He finally opened the door, and his eyes took in the room. A nurse sat by the side of the bed, watching a heart monitor.

What he saw next took his breath away. His

hand went up to his mouth, but a gasp escaped anyway.

He wasn't expecting this, not at all. But it made sense to him; it made sense of everything that had happened. There *had* been a plan after all.

Seventy-four

SOMEBODY ELSE was in the hospital bed.

Not Jane. Not what he'd been expecting, and dreading.

It was *Vivienne*.

At first, Michael didn't understand, but then he did, and some of the puzzle pieces seemed to fall into place for him. It was Vivienne who was dying. *Vivienne* who he was supposed to help.

She lay there motionless. He'd never seen her like that. Her face was unnaturally pale beneath her tan, and she wore no makeup. Her hair was loose and her white roots were showing. But in a way, she looked serene and beautiful. She looked a lot like Jane, and his heart went out to her. He wanted to help, if he could. He wanted to help them both.

"Vivienne," he said. Then, to the nurse, "I'm family. Can we have a minute?"

The nurse smiled at him and stood up. "I'll be right outside. You know she had a stroke."

Vivienne opened her eyes and looked at him. Then her eyes closed again for a second or two, as if she were trying to figure something out. He spoke gently. "Vivienne, I'm here to help you. I'm Michael."

Her eyes opened, their deep blue unfaded. "Michael?" she asked in the softest voice he'd ever heard from her. "Jane's Michael?"

"Yes, Jane's Michael." He took her hand. "I wish you could see how wonderful you look," he said. "You look the way you always want to look. Beautiful."

"There's a mirror in my purse," she said.

Michael went and got it and showed Vivienne how she looked. He'd never seen her like this, so vulnerable, the child in her allowed to show.

"I've been better. And worse, I suppose. Doesn't really matter now, does it?"

"Of course it does," said Michael. "Looking well is the best revenge."

She smiled then and put a hand on top of his. "Where is my daughter? Is Jane here?" she asked. "I can't go until I see my Jane-Sweetie."

Seventy-five

WHAT IF I HADN'T MANAGED to answer the phone finally, and heard a sobbing, nearly incoherent MaryLouise tell me to get over to New York Hospital as fast as I could? After I hung up, it was almost as if I were outside my own body. I still felt awful, but I was less nauseated. Only a bit shaky and weak. I put on fresh clothes, and then it was as if I were watching someone who looked like me hurry to the lobby of her building and tell Martin the doorman to "please get me a cab."

But it was *me* who bolted from the cab in front of New York Hospital and who ran to the information desk and was told that Vivienne Margaux was in room 703.

MaryLouise was waiting by the closed door. She kissed my cheek and shook her head back and forth. Karl Friedkin was down the hall. His head was bowed, but I could see that his eyes were full of pain. "Karl was with her when it happened," said MaryLouise.

The door to my mother's room opened just then, and a woman in a white coat asked me if I was Jane. She introduced herself as my mother's neurologist. "Your mother had a stroke," she explained gently. "It happened last night at the theater. She's been asking for you."

I nodded and tried not to cry, tried to be brave, the way Vivienne would want me to be. But as I walked into the hospital room, I was suddenly shaking all over.

There was Mother, looking very pale, and very small, and not anything like herself.

And next to her, holding her hand, was Michael.

Seventy-six

MICHAEL LOOKED AT ME and gave the slightest nod and then an understanding half smile. "Hi," he whispered. "Trade places with me." He stood, and I took over the bedside chair beside Vivienne.

"Hi, Mother. It's Jane. I'm here."

My mother's head turned and her eyes met mine. She was breathing heavily. I thought she was trying to talk but couldn't, which had never happened to her before. She had no makeup on, no perfect hairstyle. She wore a regular hospital gown, and that was when I knew how bad it was. If she'd been even a fraction of her usual self, she would have fought them over wearing that gown.

Also, she seemed glad to see me.

I moved closer. "What, Mother? What is it?"

She spoke finally, and her voice was soft and gentle. "I was tough on you, Jane-Sweetie. I know that," she said. Then my mother started to cry. "I'm sorry. I'm so sorry."

"It's okay. It's all okay," I told her.

"But I did it so you'd be strong. I did it so you wouldn't have to be like me. So cold and hard and conniving. So *Vivienne Margaux*. What a terrible thing that would have been."

"Please don't talk. Just hold my hand, Mom."

She smiled. "I like it when you call me Mom."

She'd always told me that she hated it.

She took my hand, squeezed it. "Thank God, Jane-Sweetie, you're not the least bit like me. You're just as smart. So you'll be even more successful. But you'll always be kind. You'll be *Jane*. You'll do things in your own way."

And hearing this admission brought me tears, the ones I had been holding back for years. "I thought I was such a disappointment, because I wasn't like you."

"Oh, Jane-Sweetie. No, no, no. Never. You want to know something?"

"What?"

"You're the only person I ever loved, the only one. You're the love of my life."

The love of her life.

My eyes hurt from the tears, my throat and chest ached, but my mother looked the picture of peace.

And then I thought: *So this is it?* After so many years of yelling at stagehands, screaming at secretaries, fighting with investors. After the decades of ordering around maids and chauffeurs and caterers and decorators. After the acres of designer dresses and thousand-dollar shoes. After all the trips to Paris and London and Bangkok and Cairo. This is how it ends, a frail woman on a hospital bed. My mother, and me. Together at last.

"Come closer, Jane-Sweetie," she said. "I won't bite. Probably not," she added with a weak grin.

I moved so close that our faces were almost touching.

"I have a favor to ask."

"Of course, Moth—— Mom. What do you want?"

"For God's sake, make sure they bury me...in that new Galliano brocade dress. Nothing black. I look terrible in black."

I couldn't help smiling. She was Vivienne to the end, so true to herself. "The Galliano," I said. "Check."

"And one more thing, Jane."

"Yes?"

"Don't you wear black to the funeral either. Black makes most people look thinner. But for some reason it makes you look a little top-heavy."

My smile broadened. "Okay, Mom. I'll wear *pink*. I have just the dress."

"You're funny," my mother said. "You always were. *Pink* at a funeral. Please do."

I looked over at Michael. He was smiling now too.

My mother closed her eyes, and her body shivered. I hated the idea of losing her. My mom. Finally, she was my mom.

Michael stood and walked to the other side of the bed. I held one hand. Michael held the other. This was it, wasn't it? It was all happening too fast and so suddenly.

I leaned in and kissed Vivienne on her soft, smooth cheek. She smiled and opened her eyes again. A slight nod of her head told me she wanted me closer again.

"Jane, the only thing I hate about dying is saying good-bye to you. I love you so much. Good-bye, Jane-Sweetie."

"Good-bye, Mom. I love you so much too."

And then my mother gave me one last kiss to remember her by always.

Seventy-seven

AS SHE WISHED, Vivienne was buried in the Galliano dress. She looked beautiful. In fact, the entire funeral was stunning, and also touching. Why not? Vivienne had planned it down to the tiniest detail.

I wore pink. Yves Saint Laurent pink.

The service was held on Park Avenue, at St. Bart's, of course.

Two pianists played Brahms flawlessly, as if Vivienne were standing over them. Then a soloist performed show tunes from several of the musicals my mother had produced. A couple of times, the audience burst into song.

Finally, as the service ended, on a very warm spring day, we all stood and sang my mother's favorite song, "Jingle Bells." Which was so incredibly *not* Vivienne that it was perfect too. Just as she knew it would be. And I was happy for her. My mother had produced one last hit.

As we walked out of St. Bart's to the waiting limos, Michael said to me, "If they had served cocktails, this could have been a Vivienne Margaux reunion party. As it should be."

"I loved it," I said, and hugged him. "Because she would have."

Everyone who was anybody, or pretended to be, was there. Not just Elsie and MaryLouise and the people from the office. But very famous actors, directors, stagehands and choreographers, propmen and makeup artists. All there to honor my mother and her accomplishments, which were many, including raising me to be me.

My father was there with his wife, Ellie, and at age forty-eight Ellie was finally beginning to look older than thirty. Or maybe she just dressed down in honor of Vivienne.

Howard, my stepfather, was there. Sober, too. He told me that he'd never stopped loving Vivienne. "Me too, Howard. Me too," I said, and gave him a hug.

My mother's old hairdresser, One-Name Jason, was on hand. Like Vivienne, Jason was a testimony to perfect plastic surgery. And he had done my mother one final favor. He'd flown to New York from Palm Springs just to do her hair.

Even Hugh McGrath showed up. He shook my hand, hugged me as if I were an ex-wife, told me he was sorry for everything. I almost believed him, until I remembered, *Hugh is an actor.* And *Hugh is a sonofabitch.*

The graveside service at a cemetery in Westchester County was touching and brief, also according to Vivienne's explicit direction. The minister reminded us that life was much too short, that we were destined for another world beyond this one, and that no doubt Vivienne would be producing shows in heaven. Well said, but enough said.

I placed a single rose on my mother's coffin. My style. I prayed that my mom was at peace and, if she were looking down now, that everything had gone as she wanted. *I wore pink, Mom!*

Then Michael took my hand, and we began to walk.

"We have to talk," he said, and a chill went through me.

Seventy-eight

THE SUN WAS WARM AND BRIGHT, and it lit the cemetery as though it were a stage set. The greens of the trees, the vibrant colors of the flowers, everything seemed so crisp and light and right. So why was I shivering?

"Gorgeous day," I said.

"Even God wouldn't mess with Vivienne." Michael smiled. He had loosened his tie and removed his jacket. The jacket was hooked on his index finger and slung over his shoulder. Very Michael, who was always true to himself.

"So we know why I was sent back to New York," he said. "And why I had those feelings about New York Hospital, and all the rest of it."

I nodded but didn't say anything. "I was here to help your mother. I'm almost sure of it, Jane."

I stopped walking and looked at him.

"But you're *still* here."

He smiled. "Yes, I seem to be. Unless I really am your imaginary friend. It's possible."

I poked him in the stomach. "Did you feel that?"

"Oof. Yes, I did. And I cut myself shaving, quite regularly now."

There was a pause. Michael's green eyes squinted against the bright sun.

"I think I'm here because I want to be. And I'm here because you're the only person I've ever loved too. I'm here because I couldn't stand to leave you, Jane."

I turned to him again, my heart full, and we came together and kissed gently. It was perfect.

"I have questions," I said when we separated, "that must be answered."

"I don't know if I have answers. But I'll try, Jane."

"All righty, then. Let me begin with a toughie. Have you...ever talked to, you know, *God?*"

Michael nodded. "Yes. Of course I have. Many, many times. Unfortunately, He's never talked back. He. She. Whatever. Next question?"

"So you believe in—?"

Michael looked around. "Well, how else to explain...all of this? Or me, of course? Or us? Sno-cones, Pokémon, the Simpsons, the justice system in America, iPods."

"I get it. So are you an angel?"

"Sometimes. But occasionally I'm kind of devil-may-care." He grinned, and his eyes twinkled at me. "I'm just trying to be honest."

I stomped my foot. I *needed* to know about this. *"Are you an angel,* Michael?

He looked deeply into my eyes. "I honestly don't know, Jane. Guess I'm like everybody else. I don't have a clue." He took me in his arms again. "See me, feel me," he whispered. "We've made it this far."

We continued to walk.

"Michael, I have to ask you something else. This has been *really* bothering me. Are you always going to *look* the way you look right now?"

"Exceptionally handsome, wildly debonair, unkempt?"

"Pretty much, yeah."

"You mean, am I ever going to grow old, Jane?"

"Yes."

"I honestly don't know."

"Well, you have to promise me that we're not just going to grow old together. I want us to actually *look* like we're growing old together. That would mean a lot to me."

"I'll do my best to get wrinkled and stooped, and I'll drive a big black Buick."

"Thanks," I said. "I'll do the same. And how about money?" I asked. "How do you get money?"

"That's an easy one." Michael snapped his fingers. Nothing happened. He snapped again, frowning.

"That's weird," he muttered. He snapped again, and again nothing happened. "That's scary, actually. That's usually how I get spending cash. And cabs when it's raining."

He tried one more time.

"Nothing," he said. "Hmm. Cutting myself shaving is one thing. Oh well, I'll have to find work. Maybe I could be a boxer."

I poked his stomach again.

"Maybe not."

Finally, I asked the toughest question, and the one that scared me the most. "Are you going to stay with me, Michael? Or will you leave me again? Just tell me. Let me know once and for all. Is that what's going to happen?"

Seventy-nine

MICHAEL ROLLED his eyes, which made me feel slightly—only slightly—better. Then a grimace crossed his face, and he put his hand to his chest. "Jane?" he said, sounding confused. *"Jane?"* And then he crumpled onto the stone pathway where we had been walking.

"Michael!" I dropped to my knees beside him. "Michael, what's happening?! What is it?! Michael!"

"Pain...my chest," he managed.

I began to yell for help, and fortunately a few people from my mother's funeral were still there. They came running. "Call nine-one-one!" I shouted, unable to believe this was happening. "I think he's had a heart attack. Please call nine-one-one!"

I looked back at Michael and saw that he had lost color and was perspiring heavily. I loosened his tie and opened his shirt's top button, which popped off and fell onto the path. How could this be happening, how could it happen now? I thought I was going to lose it, get hysterical, and be completely useless. I wouldn't let that happen.

"Michael, help is coming. An ambulance. Hang on, okay?"

"Jane," he repeated in a whisper.

"Please don't talk."

Michael looked so pale, so incredibly sick all of a sudden, *out of nowhere.*

"We got nine-one-one," said a man in a black suit, who I recognized as someone from the funeral parlor. "They're on their way. Try to relax, sir. It's better not to talk."

"Jane," Michael said again, sounding kind of dreamy. "You have kind eyes."

I leaned in close to him. "Please, Michael. Shh."

Michael shook his head, and I thought he was going to try to push himself up, but he didn't. "Don't tell me that. I have to talk now. There are things you need to know."

I took Michael's hand and leaned in even closer. There was a crowd around us now, but it was just the two of us down there. Just us, just like always.

Michael said in a raspy whisper, "For years, I prayed that I would see you again...as a grown-up. I prayed for this to happen, Jane. I thought about it a lot, I wished it would happen. And then it did. Somebody was listening. That's amazing, isn't it?"

"Shhhh," I whispered, feeling hot tears start in my eyes. But Michael wouldn't hush.

"You are so special, Jane. Do you understand that? Do you? I have to know you do."

"Yes." I nodded and said what he wanted to hear. "I hear you. I'm special."

Michael smiled then, and for a second he looked like himself again. He had the most incredible smile, warm and gentle and loving. It was a smile that touched my heart, had touched it when I was a child.

"I had no idea how much I was going to love you...and how good it would be," he said.

He squeezed my hand tightly. "I love you, Jane. I love you. I know I said that, but I wanted to say it again. *I love you.*" Then tears came into his eyes.

"This isn't so bad," he said with an odd little smile. Then Michael's eyes closed.

Eighty

NOW, I HAVE TO TELL YOU that what happened next couldn't have happened, which, I know, must seem crazy given what *has* happened already. But here goes.

An ambulance brought Michael to Northern Westchester Hospital. I followed close behind in a police car. A very kind doctor named John Rodman told me that Michael had blockage in all four arteries to his heart and that he would be going in for an immediate angioplasty. Heart surgery was also a possibility. The doctor wanted to know things about Michael that I simply didn't know, like how old he was and whether he had had trouble with his heart before.

Then the doctor was gone, and I was alone in the waiting room. Soon other people started to drift in, looking as nervous and uncomfortable as I was sure I did.

Now here's where it gets *really* strange.

One of the other women in the room—sandy blond hair, midthirties, very likable, even at a glance—got up for a drink of water from the fountain and then came over to me.

"May I sit?" she asked. I nodded numbly, and she took the chair next to me. "I'm a friend of Michael's," she said, which made my head jerk up. I looked into her kind, open face. "We all are." She gestured to the other people in the waiting room, who looked over at me and nodded warmly. "We're *that* kind of friend. Imaginary?"

"Oh." I was speechless for a moment, looking around at all of them and then back at the woman. "I'm Jane."

"Yes, I know. Well, Jane, we all love Michael. How is he? Do you know what's going on?"

"There's blockage to his heart," I said. "Four arteries."

The woman shook her head. "That...too strange. I'm Blythe, by the way."

"It's not strange considering what he eats," I said wryly.

She gave a little smile. "But, Jane, we don't get

sick. None of us. Ever. So yes, it is strange. Something totally unexpected, totally bizarre, is happening here."

I thought about our doomed love affair and shook my head. "You have no idea."

Blythe took my hand in hers. She was so sweet, a perfect friend already. "Actually, I do. Michael has been talking about you. He never shuts up about you. We all approve, not that you need our approval, but we do. We've never seen Michael so happy. We like you, Jane."

So we sat together, Blythe and I—my new imaginary friend—and we waited, fretted, and were scared. Finally, Dr. Rodman appeared and headed my way. There was no way to read his face, but he definitely wasn't smiling. I felt my own heart contract painfully, and my throat went dry.

Desperate, I turned to Blythe, and she shook her head. "The doctor can't see us."

Oh, okay. Of course not. I'm the only crazy person here with imaginary friends. At thirty-two years old.

"Jane," said Dr. Rodman. "Can you come with me? This is a little strange. Please, come."

Eighty-one

MICHAEL WATCHED JANE as she walked into the recovery room with his doctor. Now this was another new one—*his doctor.* Michael had never been sick a day in his life, had never been examined by a physician, certainly had never had a heart procedure. And, oh, one more thing: He'd never been frightened out of his mind like this before.

Not about dying: He was all right with that, more or less. Cautiously optimistic anyway.

But he had just found Jane again, and he didn't want to lose her for any reason. He *couldn't* lose Jane.

"Hi," she said, and he smiled weakly. He adored the sound of her voice.

"Hi. I must look like I was hit by a speeding truck. I feel like it."

"You look terrific. For somebody who was hit by a truck."

The doctor gave Jane a pat on the shoulder and left. Jane came over to Michael's bed and leaned in and kissed his forehead—and suddenly he remembered doing the exact same thing to her when she was eight. He reminded her.

"We're on the same wavelength, Michael. Of course I *remember,*" Jane said, and smiled. "I told you that I would never forget you."

Then they held hands, all four of their hands entwined together.

"Your doctor is in mild shock because you came out of the anesthesia so fast. Like, *too* fast."

Michael shrugged. "Don't know why. But what happened to me?"

Jane smiled again, and Michael felt better. "What happened to you is too much rich food, too much junk food, for God only knows how long. And I mean that quite literally. But here's the good news."

"I'm listening."

"You have a *heart,* Michael. You could have died. You're human, Michael. *You are human.*" Her face was lit with an inner joy.

"So let me see if I have this right," said Michael. "The big whoop about being human is that you get to die?"

"Live and die," Jane said. "But yeah, that's pretty much it. The big whoop."

And then Michael and Jane were both crying and hanging on to each other fiercely.

"This," he finally managed to say, "what happened today, *is* a miracle."

Eighty-two

WHILE WE'RE ON THE SUBJECT of miracles, consider this one:

Just because life is hard, and always ends in a bad way, doesn't mean that all stories have to, even if that's what they tell us in school and in the *New York Times Book Review*. In fact, it's a good thing that stories are as different as we are, one from another.

So here's how this one ends: *happily,* I should warn you.

Huge spotlights rake the night sky of Manhattan, signaling that this is a really big deal. People are waving pens and pieces of papers, screaming for autographs from the actors. Police hold back the crowd at Sixth Avenue and 54th Street. It's pretty cool. It's a genuine rush.

My stomach is all in knots, and I smile as if it isn't and walk past the paparazzi into the theater.

I'm wearing a red satin dress. It's a little snug at my hips and flares at the bottom. But I look good, and I know it. Sort of. In my own way of knowing these things and feeling good about myself, which I'm slowly getting a lot better at.

As I walk down the aisle to my seat, I can almost hear my mother saying, "Oh, Jane-Sweetie, a fancy dress like that deserves better jewelry. Why didn't you go to my vault and pick out something nice? You look so...incomplete."

I almost say out loud, "Mother, please, *not tonight.*"

I slide into the third row, all by my lonesome. That's all right, though. I can handle it. I'm a grown-up.

Then I see Michael. He looks dashing, as he *dashes* down the aisle and sits in the empty seat next to mine. "Made it," he says.

"I'm a nervous wreck," I tell him, as if he didn't know.

He gives me a hug, and my nerves instantly calm. Slightly. He's comforting, sexy, sweet—all in one.

"Okay, now I'm a nervous wreck who's wildly in love with a man who may or may not be real."

Michael pokes me lightly in the side—the poke is our thing these days. "Okay, you're real," I say.

The houselights finally dim, and the movie begins.

People in the audience cheer immediately, but I

know they're all with the studio and PR agencies, so it doesn't count.

"They love it!" Michael says.

"It hasn't started."

A title card fills the screen: "Jane Margaux, in association with ViMar Productions, presents *Thank Heaven*." More cheering, much appreciated.

I lean toward Michael and say, "The music sounds fabulous, anyway." Violins and a little soft brass.

Just right to introduce the first scene of this nice, light comedy.

A camera moves through a crowd, then in tight on a table at the Astor Court of the St. Regis Hotel. The scene was really shot at the St. Regis.

An adorable little girl sits at the table. The camera lingers on her for a moment, lets us get to know her. Apple-red cheeks. An irresistible smile.

Then the camera continues across and catches her companion, a handsome man, maybe thirty years old. Hard to tell for sure. But he's definitely a star.

"So what'll it be?" he asks.

"You know," the girl says.

"I know. Coffee ice cream with hot fudge sauce."

The actor playing the part is perfect for the role. He's an unknown, whom I just happened to discover. Plus, he needed the work.

It's Michael—playing Michael. Who else could it possibly be?

I watch him up on the screen as I hold his hand in the audience, and I think that everything in life is kind of unreal, isn't it?

And then I'm thinking—is it so impossible to imagine or believe?—that a man and a woman can find happiness together for a little while, which, after all, is all that we have. All anyone has.

I think it can happen. It happened to me, to Jane-Sweetie, so it can probably happen to anybody.

By the way, the movie audience loved *Thank Heaven*.

Strawberries with Whipped Cream

Eighty-three

MICHAEL WAS SEATED at a table in the Astor
Court at the St. Regis, with an absolutely adorable
four-year-old girl named Agatha, who preferred to
be called Aggie.

Aggie was Michael's latest mission, and although
he always tried to do something fresh and new with
every one of his kids, he couldn't resist the St. Regis
on a Sunday afternoon. This place was all about good
memories, right?

The waiter placed a bowl of melon balls and
lemon sherbet in front of him.

"Thanks so much," said Michael, as if the waiter
had done him a great favor, which Michael believed
he had, since he did his job so well.

The waiter had already given Aggie her sundae—
strawberries with whipped cream, over strawberry
ice cream, with a dab of strawberry jam.

"You're such a *girl*," Michael kidded her.

"I *am* a girl, silly," said Aggie, who had the most amazing smile to go with her beautiful green eyes.

Michael was tempted to teach her something that he would call the Aggie-and-Michael game, but he resisted this urge. He needed something even better for Aggie—and here it came now.

"Aggie, *look!*"

Jane had taken their one-year-old son, Jack, to the restroom, and the two of them had just reentered the Astor Court and were now hurrying across the restaurant. Jack was pointing at the ceiling, and exclaiming, "Yite, yite," which was his word for "light," or anything else that he liked a lot.

"Here come Mommy and Jack!" Michael exclaimed, and he felt his heart spike with excitement, as it always did. He felt so lucky, so fortunate, so *blessed*, to have Jane, and to have this family.

"Now we can play monkey in the middle," said Aggie, laughing. "And you're the monkey, Daddy. Okay?"

"Okay," said Michael, "except that we need a ball for that game. But of course I'm the monkey. I'm the hairy, homely one, aren't I?" Then he turned to Jane, smiled, and whispered—just for her—"I missed you. I always miss you."

"I missed you too. But now I'm here," said Jane.

"We're all here, the four of us. And there's nothing in the world that's better than that. Nothing I could imagine in my wildest dreams."

Jane sat down at her place and dipped a spoon into her sundae—hot fudge over coffee ice cream—and gave Jack the first taste of this delicious confection.

"Yite!" the little boy exclaimed.

With affection,

James Patterson
Gabrielle Charbonnet

About the Authors

JAMES PATTERSON published his first thriller in 1976 and since then has become one of the best-known and bestselling writers of all time, with more than 140 million copies of his books sold worldwide. He is the author of the two most popular detective series of the past decade, featuring Alex Cross and the Women's Murder Club, and he has written numerous other #1 bestsellers. He has won an Edgar Award—the mystery world's highest honor—and his novels *Kiss the Girls* and *Along Came a Spider* were made into feature films starring Morgan Freeman. His charity, the James Patterson PageTurner Awards, has given hundreds of thousands of dollars to individuals and groups that promote the excitement of books and reading. He lives in Florida.

GABRIELLE CHARBONNET also writes children's books. She lives in North Carolina with her husband, two daughters, two stepsons, a poodle, and an unfortunate number of cats.

Reading Group Guide

Discussion Questions

1. So many New York City landmarks lend atmosphere to this novel: the St. Regis Hotel, the Metropolitan Museum of Art, Central Park, the Cathedral of St. John the Divine, and, of course, Tiffany's. If the novel were set in your town, what local landmarks would it feature? Do you think this novel would be as interesting if it were set somewhere else?

2. Michael says that the role of an imaginary friend is to make children feel less alone and to help them find their place in the world. Do you think imaginary friends help children deal with their lives or keep them from dealing with life head-on? In what other ways do we use our imagination to cope with life or hide from it?

3. When Michael leaves Jane on her ninth birthday, Jane is devastated and says, "I'll never forget you Michael, no matter what." Do you think there is one perfect love for each of us? How influenced are we by portrayals of love and love affairs in the media, movies, and on television?

Reading Group Guide

4. Jane is involved in an unfulfilling relationship with Hugh McGrath. Is it surprising that without a good role model for loving relationships from her own parents, she would find herself staying in a bad relationship? With so many of us coming from divorced homes, how can we break the cycle and have successful love relationships?

5. Jane's play, *Thank Heaven,* is based on her childhood friendship with Michael. Would you have an interest in seeing the play? Do you prefer the play's ending where Michael leaves on Jane's ninth birthday or do you prefer the book's ending where Jane and Michael meet again as adults?

6. Jane's special emergency feel-good food is Oreos. Do you have a favorite comfort food? Is it good to avoid your favorite foods or does that just lead to more bingeing behavior? How can you help children so they develop healthy relationships with food?

7. Jane "gifts herself" with a diamond ring from Tiffany's to wear on her right hand. The salesperson assures her that more and more women are buying them. If you could afford a $65,000 diamond for yourself, would you like one? If a woman does not have a man in her life, do you think it is an empowering act for her to buy her own diamond ring?

8. Michael explains to Jane that when children turn nine years old, their imaginary friends must leave them. But he recalls that when Jane was just four, she told him, "Love means you can never be apart." Does this statement from Jane explain why they don't forget each other? How do you explain it?

9. Michael gives up his immortality to be with Jane. Do you think he could have made another choice? Do you support his decision? If you had been presented with a similar situation, what would you have done to be with the one you loved?

10. Michael takes Jane to Nantucket because he doesn't want to waste a minute of the time they have together. Michael says, "Is it so difficult to imagine or believe that a man and a woman can find happiness together for a little while, which, after all, is all that we have?" Is this the moral of the story for you? If not, what is?

Either with a reading group or on your own, please feel free to share answers with the author at www.jamespatterson.com.

James Patterson's
READKIDDOREAD.com

Dear Reader,

My true passion lies in getting people of all ages genuinely excited about books and reading. I believe that reading can be every bit as captivating as a blockbuster film or as interactive and addictive as a video game — *if you give people books they're going to love.*

My latest project is a Web site called READ KIDDO READ, which will help parents, grandparents, mentors, and adults everywhere find truly great reads for kids.

It's an easy-to-use Web site that will make picking a book easier and more effective by culling through the overwhelming options available and suggesting great books that kids will gobble up, then ask for more.

Sharing books you love can and should be a family affair. That's why I've also created THE JAMES PATTERSON PAGE-TURNERS, which are, in the spirit of the most enduring hit movies and books, action-packed stories for readers ages 10 to 110.

The first PAGETURNER series is the Maximum Ride novels. Reading these books together can provoke lively discussions about important issues, including global warming, genetics and biotechnology, leadership, friendship, and much more.

Starting on the next page is a preview of the latest book in the Maximum Ride series, *MAX*. Please share and discuss it with the children in your life.

Happy reading!

Chapter Four

I'M NOT A great sleeper. When you've spent your whole
life facing imminent pain and death, you tend not to sink too
deeply into the arms of Morpheus. So it was nothing new that
I lay awake for hours that night, turning this way and that.

I know what you're wondering: How do the wings fit into
the whole sleeping thing? Well, we're not back sleepers. Our
wings fold up neatly and tightly along our spines, but it isn't
comfortable to be stuck on our backs for any length of time.
So we're mostly side or stomach sleepers. Little bit of insider
bird kid info for ya there.

Right now I was flopped on my stomach, my head hanging off the side of the bed I was sharing with Angel. Nudge
had won the "Flock Member Most Likely to Cause Injuries by
Kicking During Sleep" award last year, so she got a bed to
herself.

My wings were unfolded a bit, and I reached around to
pull a twig out of my secondaries. Here's what I was thinking
about:

1) Who this new threat was
2) The air show in Mexico City
3) My mom and my half-sister, Ella
4) How to get Total to quit milking his tail injury, because
   enough was enough
5) Fang
6) Fang
7) Fang

I'd grown up with Fang, from the very beginning, when our dog crates were stacked next to each other in the lab of experimental horror that we called the School. I know, just another typical romantic story about the boy next door.

Then we'd been rescued by our bad-guy-turned-good-turned-bad-again-turned-I-don't-know-what-lately, and Fang and I had been like brother and sister with the rest of the flock, hidden away in the Colorado mountains.

Then Jeb had disappeared and I had become flock leader. Maybe because I was the oldest. Or the most ruthless. Or the most organized. I don't know. But I was the flock leader, and Fang was my right-wing man.

This past year, things had started to change. Fang had been interested in a girl (see Red-Haired Wonder, book two), and I'd hated it. I'd had my first date with a guy (possibly evil, but not sure), and Fang had hated it. Then, last month, he'd gotten all cozy with Dr. Brigid Dwyer, the twenty-year-old scientist who'd been part of the research team down in the land of ice and snow and killer leopard seals. And—get this—she'd sort of flirted back with him. And he's only fourteenish!

In between all this, Fang had kissed me. Several times. So now I was freaked and tempted and terrified and worried and longing and also angry at him for even starting this whole thing to begin with. But it was started and couldn't be unstarted. (Again, his fault.) And now I was trying to brush my hair, you know, when I thought about it, and looking at myself in mirrors, wondering if I was pretty. Pretty! A year ago, when my hair got in my eyes, I hacked it off with a knife. The only thing important about my clothes was whether they were too stiff with *whatever* to move fast in battle. And Fang had been my best friend and an excellent fighter.

Now everything was upside down.

"You *are* really pretty, Max," said a small voice next to me.

I pressed my face into my pillow and squelched some extra-colorful words. Way to go, ace—have embarrassing personal thoughts while you're *two feet* from a *mind reader*. Yes. Along with the wings and the raptor eyesight and the weird bones, etc., the insane scientists who'd created us had included the whimsy of suddenly developing other skills.

Iggy can feel colors. Nudge can attract metal stuff to her and hack any computer. Fang can pretty much disappear into whatever background he's against. I can fly faster than the others, and I have a Voice in my head. I don't want to talk about that right now. Gazzy can imitate any voice, any sound, with 100 percent accuracy. His other skill is unmentionable. But it was Angel who'd hit the genetic jackpot. She can breathe underwater, communicate with animals, and read people's minds. We're talking about a six-year-old. And, you know, six-year-olds are *famous* for having excellent *judgment* and *decision-making skills*.

"You have nice hair and really pretty eyes," Angel went on earnestly.

I rolled over a bit. "Yeah. Brown and brown." Have I mentioned how much Fang loves *red* hair? I believe I have.

"No, your hair has little sun streaks in it," Angel informed me. "And your eyes are like—you know those chocolates we had in France? With the gooey stuff in the middle, with the alcohol in 'em except we didn't know, and Gazzy ate a million of them and then barfed all night? Those chocolates?"

As much as I had tried to suppress all memory of that incident, it rushed back to me in vivid Technicolor. "The color of my eyes is like barfed-up chocolate?" Despair settled over me. There was no hope.

"No, the chocolates before they were barfed," Angel said.

So there you have it, the extent of my charms: brown hair and eyes like unbarfed chocolate. I'm a lucky girl.

"Max," said Angel, "you know Fang is the best guy ever. And he loves you. 'Cause you're the best girl ever."

With anyone else, I could have asked them how they knew

that, and then discredit them. Not with Angel. She knew because she'd seen it, in his mind.

"We all love each other, Ange," I said impatiently, hating this whole conversation.

"No, not like this," she went on relentlessly. "Fang loves you."

Here's a little secret you might not have picked up on about me: I can't stand gushy emotion. Hate crying. Hate feeling sad. Am not even too crazy about feeling happy. So all this—the vulnerability, the longing, the terror—I desperately wanted it all to go away forever. I wanted to cut it out of me like that chip in my arm. (See book three; I can't keep explaining everything. If I'm gonna take the trouble to write this stuff down, the least you can do is read it.) But right now I needed to shut Angel up.

"Okay, maybe I'll give him a break," I said, rolling over and closing my eyes.

"Maybe you should give him more than that," Angel pressed.

My eyes flared open as I didn't dare to think what she might mean.

"He could totally be your boyfriend," she went on with annoying persistence. "You guys could get married. I could be like a junior bridesmaid. Total could be your flower dog."

"I'm only fourteen!" I said. "Probably! I can't get married!"

"You could in New Hampshire."

My mouth dropped open. How does she know this stuff? "Forget it! No one's getting married!" I hissed. "Not in New Hampshire or anywhere else! Not in a box, not with a fox! Now go to sleep, *before I kill you*!"

Oh yeah, like I got any sleep after *that*.

Chapter Five

YOU'VE NEVER SEEN just how mega a megalopolis can be until you've seen Mexico City. I guess there might be bigger burgs in, like, China or something, but boy howdy, Mexico City seemed endless.

Anyway, the Bane of My Existence and I had agreed to one more air show, and of course it was the one in Mexico City, where Dr. Wonderful would be meeting us.

So we were over a ginormous open-air stadium, the Estadio Azteca, which held about 114,000 people. Every seat was filled. We'd changed the choreography and order of stunts since the last show, so if anyone had made a plan to take us out, they'd have to rethink it. Around us, mile upon mile of densely packed buildings stretched as far as we could see, and we can see pretty dang far.

"I need a scuba tank," Nudge said, flying over to me. She was holding her nose with one hand. "And a face mask." She gave a couple of coughs and shook her head, her eyes watering.

"I assume you're referring to the wee pollution problem?" I said, raising my voice to be heard over the wind, and over the multitudes cheering below. The people in the stadium were looking up to see us silhouetted against a thick, gray sky. And it was not cloudy today. The thing is, with nineteen million–plus people and four million–plus cars and a bunch of businesses making stuff, Mexico City is incredibly, horribly, nauseatingly polluted.

Which was why the CSM wanted us to be here—to bring international attention to it. When Dr. Wonderful was prepping us for the air show, she'd told us that there had been over half-a-million pollution-related hospital cases just in the past year. That's a lot of smog.

"I'm getting a headache," Gazzy said, circling closer to me.

We split apart in a six-pointed star, with Total in the middle, and the crowd below went crazy. Like a huge, rolling wave of sound, the chants came to us:

"We have the power! The future is now! Kids rule!"

I raised an eyebrow at Fang. " 'Kids rule'?"

He shrugged. "I can't control what they quote from the blog," he said. "What am I gonna say? 'More power to grown-ups'? I don't think so."

"How many readers do you have now?"

Fang had started a blog months ago, using our super-duper contraband computer. He had his own fan clubs and everything. Girls sent him ridiculous e-mails about how wonderful he was, what a hero, etc. It was enough to turn your stomach.

"About six hundred thousand log in pretty much every day," Fang said, automatically scanning the airspace around us. He and I suddenly soared upward, facing each other, about two feet apart. The crowd below gasped, and I knew it looked impressive as all get-out. Then Iggy zoomed up to join us, and he, Fang, and I made a triangle, our wings moving in perfect order so that we didn't whap one another on the upstroke.

A hundred yards below us, Nudge, Gazzy, and Angel were a triple stack of bird kids, centered directly over one another, moving their wings in unison, everyone up, everyone down. At a signal, they all turned and started rocketing earthward, still precisely stacked.

Fang, Iggy, and I counted to ten, then angled downward also: It was time for us to land on the field—supposedly they were going to give us some kind of award.

"You're national heroes," Dr. Amazing had said earlier, pushing her—yes—*red* hair out of her eyes while Fang watched her with interest. "Not only here, but in other countries, too. You guys are so young, but you've accomplished so much, and exposed so much evil. Plus, you helped publicize the melting of Antarctica's ice cap and spoke in Congress. You're amazing."

Who was she beaming at? Yes. Fang.

Who, exactly, had gotten up the guts to speak to Congress? That would be *moi*. But judging from Brigid Dwyer's unprofessional adoration, Fang alone had just saved the entire known world with one wing tied behind his back.

It had been all I could do to not trip Brigid on her way out. Which was stupid, because why did I even care? Never mind. Forget I asked. I don't want to talk about it.

Moving on. The field below, big enough for the World Cup, the Olympics, and anything else where 114,000 people all suddenly needed to be in the same place at the same time, beckoned us. There was a line of uniformed security guards hired by the CSM ringing the field to protect us. I saw Nudge, Gazzy, and Angel land flawlessly and then separate, waving at the crowd as a hundred thousand cameras flashed.

Unfortunately, since a camera's flash bears a striking resemblance to the flash a gun makes when it's fired, by the time I landed on the green turf, I was so twitchy and pumped full of adrenaline that I felt like I might hurl.

We landed and all automatically circled, our backs to one another, as if we were six cute little covered wagons warding off the Indians who were inexplicably pissed that we'd taken all their land and given them all colds and killed most of them off.

The crowd was roaring too loudly for us to hear guns. Heck, we wouldn't have been able to hear a chopper. It was pretty much the most nightmarish situation I could possibly imagine, without it literally involving a dog crate.

And you know what's coming, right?

Yeah. The actual nightmare part.

Chapter Six

THE SETTING: AN impossibly big open stadium in impressive but noxious Mexico City.

The cast of characters: the flock, Total, Dr. Amazing, and some very nice Mexican officials who wanted to give us an award. Plus a TV crew.

The plot: Just wait. It's coming.

"I HATE THIS. Get me outta here," I said to Fang, keeping a smile stuck on my face. We were waving to the crowd, so many camera flashes going off that I would be blind in a minute.

"This is not a good setup," Fang agreed, looking around constantly.

Total, Iggy, Gazzy, and Nudge were working the crowd like old hands, bowing and soaking up the applause. Gazzy was giving little six-foot hops into the air, spreading his wings, and each time, the crowd roared even louder.

Finally, one of the officials tapped on a microphone set up in the center of the stadium. Brigid Dwyer stood next to them, ready to give a speech about the CSM and what it was trying to accomplish worldwide.

The official said something in Spanish, and the crowd cheered and clapped, chanting quotes from Fang's blog. Then Brigid took the microphone and waited for relative quiet.

"Buenos días, señors y señoras," Brigid said, and people cheered. "Hoy, nosotros—"

Right then, a piercing scream soared over the crowd's murmur, stopping Brigid cold. Gazzy saw them first: Eraser-type thingies leaping over the upper ledge of the stadium and rappelling down to the field.

"Heads up!" Fang shouted. We had a second to exchange glances, thinking the same thing: We hadn't seen them on the roof, just minutes before. Where had they come from?

"Up and away!" I yelled to the flock, then saw the problem: Brigid couldn't fly out with us. We couldn't leave her to the Erasers' mercy, or lack thereof. We couldn't abandon her and the rest of the people who had hosted us.

The officials, Brigid, and the TV crew gazed openmouthed as at least sixty slim, dark figures hit the ground and headed for us. I summed up the situation in an instant: a hundred thousand people who might be injured or killed in cross fire; innocent people right here on the field who would only get in our way; the six and a half of us up against about sixty of the "New Threat" things.

It was like old times.

"Belay that!" I shouted. "Battle up!"

As a maternal figure, I always wanted what was best for the flock, to keep it safe, to do my best to get it what it needed. But I admit it did my heart proud to see the instant bloodlust pop into Gazzy's blue eyes, to see little Angel automatically tense up and get into fighting stance, ready to rip someone's head off. They were just so — so dang *adorable* sometimes.

We were a tiny bit out of practice — I hadn't taken anyone apart in several weeks. But once you've learned the nasty, street-fighting, no-holds-barred art of Max Kwon Do, you never really forget it.

"Get 'em!" I shouted as the dark figures raced toward us. Liquid-fire adrenaline surged into my veins, making me jittery and lightning fast.

As soon as one was within striking range, I jumped up and out, both feet forward. They connected heavily, slamming the New Threat in its middle. It doubled over but snapped upright quickly, its dark hood slipping back to reveal a weird, humanish face. Humanish except for the glowy green eyes like lasers.

I landed, spun on one heel, and snap-kicked backward as hard as I could. I caught it in the shoulder and heard a crunching, breaking sound. With its good arm it swung at my head, much faster than a human could, and with more force. I leaped back just in time, feeling the barest brush of its knuckles against my cheek. A second one rushed up, followed by a third. One grabbed me from behind, tearing my jacket—my new jacket that my mom had given me. Brand-new, not from Goodwill or a Dumpster. He'd *torn* it.

Now I was mad. A split-second glance revealed that the flock was doing what it did best: deconstructing things. No one needed help, so I balled my fists, put my head down, and went after my attackers.

These things always seemed to last much longer than they actually did. I felt as though I was punching and kicking and swinging and whaling for two hours, but it was probably about six minutes or so. These New Threat thingies had a couple of vulnerable spots: If you brought both hands down in a chopping motion right on top of their heads, their heads actually split open into several metallic strips, like an Easter egg. Okay, a really gross Easter egg, but you get the idea.

Another vulnerable spot: their trim little ankles. One good strong kick and they'd snap like balsa wood.

In less than ten minutes, thanks to us and the hired security force, the grassy lawn looked like a combination of an army field hospital and an automobile chop shop. Brigid and the officials were white-faced, huddled together by the podium. A quick inventory of the flock revealed the usual bruises, bloody noses, and black eyes, but nothing serious.

Fang came up, his face grim, his knuckles raw and bleeding.

I knew what he was going to say. "Okay, no more air shows," I admitted.

Chapter Seven

DR. DWYER AND the CSM had organized a special safe house for us—actually, they had organized five, and kept the final choice a secret until we were in a car headed there.

"It's hard if you're not used to it," Fang said, watching Brigid's white face. She nodded tensely, working hard to maintain her cool. She hadn't been hurt, but her clothes were spattered with blood—I'd been standing right next to her when I had happily discovered the New Threat's Easter egg weakness.

"It's not a picnic even if you *are* used to it," I said.

"What were those things?" Iggy asked, rubbing his bruised and scraped knuckles.

"Not sure," I said. I'd been trying to figure that out myself. They hadn't been Erasers, those wolf-human hybrids that had tried to kill us about once every hour for the past four years. They hadn't been Flyboys, which were the flying, cyborg version of Erasers. They hadn't been straight robots. They were roboty, but with a bit of flesh grown over their frame, and apparently didn't fly. They hadn't spoken, but that didn't mean they couldn't.

"It's a mystery," I said, deciding to worry about it later. Right now I was hungry and a little shaky from the adrenaline comedown. I pushed my hair out of my eyes, and just then noticed that Dr. Brilliant's hair was actually cut in a style, like on purpose. I'd had my hair cut by an actual haircut person exactly once in my life, and that was many, many battles ago.

I felt like a truck driver next to Brigid Dwyer. A truck driver with bad hair, a black eye, dried blood around my nose, and ripped and bloody clothes. Not an unusual look for me, but all of a sudden, I felt—I don't know. I don't know what I felt.

"Here we are," said Brigid as we pulled into the driveway of a smallish stucco house. The houses were packed tightly together here, and the streets were full of dogs and cars, the yards hung with laundry lines holding clean laundry. I automatically scanned the area for possible hiding places, points of vulnerability, whether the windows were breakable, whether the trees would get in our way. I felt tired and irritable, and worse, I kept sensing Fang looking at Brigid. I just wanted to eat about three banana splits and then get into a hot shower.

Fang got out first, raked the area with his stare, and determined that it was safe. The rest of us piled out quickly and hurried to the back of the house. Warm yellow light spilled out a window in a slanted rectangle on the grass. Just as we reached the back door, it opened. I stopped so suddenly that Angel ran into me. I got on the balls of my feet, ready to leap into action if someone dangerous was behind that door.

It swung open and at first all I saw was a silhouette. At the same moment, a delicious, familiar scent wafted out into the warm night air.

Chocolate-chip cookies, fresh from the oven.

The silhouette was my mom, Dr. Valencia Martinez, and she was smiling at me.

And the world seemed loads better.